I0682116

Jill's Ponies:

Black Boy and Rapide

by Jemma Spark

Book Eight of Jemma Spark's Jill Series

Epona Publishing

www.ponybookuniversc.com

Copyright © 2021 by Jemma Spark

The moral right of the author has been asserted.

All rights reserved.

No part of this publication may be reproduced, stored in a retrieval system, or transmitted in any form or by any means, without the prior permission in writing of the author, nor be otherwise circulated in any form of binding or cover other than that in which it is published and without a similar condition including this condition being imposed on the subsequent purchaser.

Trade paperback ISBN 978-0-6450263-7-5

Jill Books

Table of Contents

Cast of Characters

HUMANS

Agnes Pevensy - known to all as 'Aggie', the Duchess of Tolkington, lives at Pevensy Park and is a life-long horse-mad woman with five children.

Angela - a young girl who rides her own pony Christie for riding lessons at Mrs Darcy's riding school, a member of the Birtle Pony Club.

Ann Derry – famous for being Jill Crewe's best friend, currently studying at college so that she can gain entry to Bristol Veterinary College next year. Her boyfriend is Henry Thurston, the local vet. She lives at Pool Cottage.

April Cholly-Sawcutt – once as round as a bouncing ball, she is now slim, the eldest of the three Cholly-Sawcutt sisters, the daughter of Captain Cholly-Sawcutt, engaged to Gary Horton, who is running her father's showjumping yard.

Austin Pevensy – the second eldest son, younger brother of Royce and Mercedes, and older brother of Porsche and Morgan. Attends Lonsdale College at Oxford, a good rider who competes in point-to-points and hunter trials. Doesn't take anything seriously, good-humoured and glamorous.

Barty King – married to Susan Pyke, a solicitor in a Rychester firm, his sole ambition to be a partner in the firm.

Bert Munro – stable manager at Pevensy Park stables.

Beryl Tainton – friend of Aggie Pevensy, rides in show hunter classes.

Captain Cholly-Sawcutt – once competed on the international showjumping stage representing Britain, now has dementia.

Charlie Moreton – husband of Clarissa, owns a jump racing stable near Cambridge.

Claire – long-suffering maid of the Ellison-Heaths, forced to wear a ridiculous black and white uniform.

Clarissa Moreton (née Dandleby) – one of Cecilia's friends (Cecilia is Jill's cousin), she has married one of her father's friends called Charlie Morton, who runs a jump racing stable.

Mrs Darcy – ran the local Chatton riding school in all the original Jill books but has been away for some time leaving Wendy Mead in charge.

Mrs Derry – Ann Derry's mother, a worrier.

Diana Bush – a lifelong friend of Ann and Jill, the sister of James, a good rider but not ambitious in the equestrian field

Dinah Dean – one of the original characters in the Jill books, a determined young girl who rescued the ponies that were going to slaughter, adopted by Mrs Whirley at Blossom Park and is now studying law at university, an anti-blood sports advocate.

Dougie – a young boy of unprepossessing appearance with a huge nose, wide-blown nostrils and pancake freckles. Owns a grey pony of Welsh and Arab breeding and has lessons at Mrs Darcy's riding school.

Mr Ellison-Heath – the husband of Evelyn Ellison-Heath and the father of Lavender, works for an insurance company in Oxford.

Evelyn Ellison-Heath – mother of Lavender Ellison-Heath, desperate to climb the social ladder in local society, godmother of Susan King (née Pyke), shares Mrs Pyke's passion for spiky hot-house plants.

The Miss Farthingtons (Felicia and Jessica) – a pair of eccentric elderly sisters who keep a menagerie of animals in their large house, including Patchwork, a skewbald gelding eventer who lives in the dining room.

Frank Stabley – a local showjumper from Chatton, currently in America working for a horsey family.

Gary Horton – an up and coming showjumper who is engaged to April Cholly-Sawcutt and running her father's showjumping yard.

George Pyke – a robust country gentleman, the father of Susan King, has a stable full of horses and enjoys going hunting with his cronies.

Henry Thurston – the local vet, competitor in point-to-points and hunter trials, boyfriend of Ann Derry.

Mrs Hipkiss – the chairman of the cottage hospital fund-raising committee.

Jackie Heath – a lifelong friend of Ann and Jill, the twin sister of Val who is currently in America working as a riding instructor.

James Bush – lifelong friend of Ann and Jill, brother of Diana, committed to point-to-pointing and steeplechasing.

Jill Crewe – the author of the famous Jill books.

June Cholly-Sawcutt – the youngest of the three Cholly-Sawcutt sisters who are the daughters of Captain Cholly-Sawcutt.

May Cholly-Sawcutt – the middle one of the three Cholly-Sawcutt sisters who are the daughters of Captain Cholly-Sawcutt.

Lavender Ellison-Heath – an eleven-year-old girl who is the proud owner of Jill's pony Black Boy, attends a private day school in Birtle.

Louis Pevensy - the Duke of Tolkington, the acquiescent husband of Aggie, father of five children, has a passion for motor cars.

Mercedes Pevensy – the eldest daughter of Aggie and Louis, utterly gorgeous looking, a good rider and serious and conscientious eventer with heavy weight aspirations.

Mrs Milner – the Pevensy Cook.

Morgan Pevensy – an eleven-year-old girl, the youngest of the five Pevensy children.

Miss Penwith – retired Pevensy nanny.

Miss Pomfret – judge of riding classes at Chatton Show in 1963, reputed to always prefer chestnuts and won't look at blacks.

Porsche Pevensy – a seventeen-year-old young woman, the fourth of the five Pevensy children, a wild child, a very good rider and desperately ambitious, suffers from crushing sibling rivalry with her older sister, Mercedes.

Mrs Pyke – wife of George, mother of Susan, loves spiky hothouse flowers.

Royce Pevensy – the eldest Pevensy child, will inherit the title and be a Duke when his father dies, writes poetry, likes riding but concentrates on managing the Pevensy Park estate.

Ruby Swope – young girl who is a helper at Mrs Darcy's riding school, lives in Ditching Hollow in a caravan, very enthusiastic young horsewoman, not backwards in coming forwards.

Serena – the riding instructor at Mrs Darcy's riding school.

Susan King (née Pyke) – a main character in the original Jill books, she would openly scoff at Jill when she was first learning to ride and hung around with a crew of like-minded girls who followed her lead, she has recently married Bartholomew King, a local solicitor, and lives in a new house in a development on the outskirts of Rychester.

Ted - a young boy with bright red hair and large freckles across his snub nose who rides at Mrs Darcy's riding school.

Colonel Ted Motley – a retired horseman who has recently moved to Chatton and is on the organising committee of Chatton Show.

Mr Titchley – Manager of Goddards Department Store, who donated the prizes to the Blossom Park Hunter Trials.

Tom – a groom at Pevensy Park stables.

Val Heath – twin sister of Jackie Heath, lifelong friend of Jill Crewe, currently in America working as a riding instructor.

Violet – a young girl who usually rides Blackstone at Mrs Darcy's riding school.

Wendy Mead – a lifelong friend of Jill and Ann, running Mrs Darcy's riding school with hopes to become the proprietor when Mrs Darcy retires.

HORSES AND PONIES

Banjo – beautiful bay gelding, owned by Mercedes Pevensy, her best horse and prospective mount for Burghley and Badminton.

Blackstone – small black pony at Mrs Darcy's riding school.

Black Boy – 13.2 hh, aged black gelding, the most famous pony in the world of Jill, her first pony, now owned by Lavender Ellison-Heath, who for a time renamed him Bingle Jells but then reverted to his original name.

Black Comedy – ex-steeplechaser, big brown horse with a rectangular head and thick, scarred legs, previously owned by Jill Crewe, who sold him to Ann Derry, who trains him for her boyfriend, Henry Thurston.

Bright Eyes – home-bred bay gelding owned by Wendy Mead, entered in the novice horse event at Blossom Park Hunter Trials.

Christie – pale, palomino pony owned by Angela, who is a member of Birtle Pony Club.

Dauntless – chestnut gelding owned by Henry Thurston, unable to compete at Blossom Park Hunter Trials due to a leg injury.

Diablo – an evil black gelding with a malevolent nature but fast and fearless over jumps, owned by George Pyke, ridden by Susan King (née Pyke), entered in the open event at Blossom Park Hunter Trials.

Firefly – good looking chestnut gelding with four white socks and a white diamond on his forehead, owned and ridden by Austin Pevensy and entered in the open event at Blossom Park Horse Trials.

Jago – big, bay thoroughbred, owned by James Bush, entered in the open event at Blossom Park Hunter Trials.

Irish boy – grey thoroughbred, owned by James Bush, entered in the novice event at Blossom Park Hunter Trials.

Lancaster Bomber – jumper owned by James Bush, entered in the novice event at Blossom Park Hunter Trials to be ridden by James' sister, Diana.

Mangala – ungainly grey gelding, ex-racehorse bought at a sale by the Pevensys, with a view to retraining him for cross-country and eventing. Ridden by Porsche at the Blossom Park Hunter Trials.

Mousie – a small, dun pony mare at Mrs Darcy's riding school.

Patchwork – skewbald gelding belonging to the Miss Farthingtons, stabled in their dining room while he is being trained as an eventer.

Rapide – bay, 14.2 hh gelding, the second most famous pony in the world of Jill. He was her showjumper, full of character and mischievous quirks, was being ridden by Porsche Pevensy last season but now is assigned to the youngest Pevensy child, Morgan, who likes him but isn't keen on riding in general.

Red Hornet – 17.2 hh chestnut steeplechaser gelding, owned by Gary Horton and April Cholly-Sawcutt, entered in the open event at Blossom Park Hunter Trials.

Sassy Swoop –glamourous and sparkling mare with large dark eyes and perfectly shaped pointed ears, owned by Mercedes Pevensey, one of her up and coming eventers, entered in the open class at Blossom Park Hunter Trials.

Sirius – tall, brown and serious gelding, with no mischievous twists and turns in his character, owned by Mercedes Pevensey, one of her eventers, reliable but unlikely to be a champion, entered in the open class at Blossom Park Hunter Trials.

Skydiver – utterly gorgeous grey gelding, highly-trained in dressage and owned by Jill Crewe.

Totty – retired small grey gelding who served his time in Mrs Darcy's riding school for many years.

Troubadour – faithful old hunter belonging to the Pevensys.

Chapter One – Chatton Show, 1963

Lavender Ellison-Heath, the present owner of Jill Crewe's pony Black Boy, rose early on the morning of Chatton Show. Today was to be the high point of her summer, perhaps the high point of her whole life. Or, it might be the day of doom and destruction, when she would have to bow to her mother's wishes and agree that her beloved pony be traded in for a more upmarket show pony.

Lavender had renamed Black Boy as Bingle Jells. Bingle for short. He was now a venerable gentleman of fifteen years. Certainly not a has-been, but somewhat beyond the heady days of his youth. Lavender loved him with all her heart. But her mother had social aspirations and was hoping to become part of the elite County set in Oxfordshire. She believed that winning rosettes at all the County shows would put them up there with the toffs.

Lavender's mother, an irksome and unattractive woman, longed for gymkhana glory. She was determined that Lavender should be mixing with those in the winning circle and going to Richmond and Harringay. She longed for them to be established amongst the very elite of the showing world. If Bingle did not come up to scratch, they would get rid of him and acquire a top-notch pony. Lavender despaired of her mother's ignoble ambitions and was desperate to keep Bingle. She didn't care about winning blue ribbons. She loved her kind and faithful pony and was prepared to do anything to keep him.

Yesterday there had been the most tremendous thunderstorm. Lavender had been in the stable grooming Bingle when the storm had hit. Lightning had flashed, and rolls of thunder like the drumbeats of the gods had shaken the ground. This morning she ran to the window and looked out. The world was newly-washed, a golden sun in a blue sky with only tiny wisps of cloud scudding away over the horizon. It promised to be a perfect summer day.

Bingle had been washed and groomed on the previous day, then carefully swathed in a clean summer rug so that he didn't soil himself in the night. His head was hanging over the half-stable door, his ears pricked, watching for his owner's arrival when Lavender skipped into the stable yard. It was as if he knew that today was a special day. He had been going to Chatton Show nearly every year. Jill had ridden him there with great success when she had been a young teenager.

Although Chatton showground was within easy hacking distance, Lavender's mother had insisted that they travel there in their small, flash horsebox that had been purchased recently. Mrs Ellison-Heath had to show the world that they were in the upper echelons of competitors with a very smart truck, complete with picnic table and chairs and a hamper of expensive luxuries to be offered around to any poor unfortunate who could be persuaded to join them. Lavender would squirm with embarrassment when her mother approached the other posh people who politely rebuffed her advances.

Mrs E-H had a dream of herself presiding over these impromptu equestrian social gatherings. She had heard how smart people picnicked out of their car boots at point-to-points, and she longed to become one of them. Unfortunately, she just didn't seem to have the knack for establishing social bonds. For some reason that she could not fathom, the socialites of the horsey world avoided her. The only horsey person with whom she could claim kinship was her god-daughter, Susan King, who had been Susan Pyke before she had married Barty King, a local solicitor.

Lavender had been suffering from her mother's pretensions since the day she was born, but at the age of eleven, as she became more conscious of how other people viewed her mother, it was becoming harder and harder to bear. Mrs E-H was everything manicured and lacquered. She regularly had her hair rinsed and set, dyed a most unlikely shade of platinum blonde, with little twisted curls that framed her hard face. Her eyebrows were firmly etched in long, elongated curves and her thin mouth lipsticked in strong colours. The way she spoke made one shudder, like when fingers are scratched down a blackboard. Her voice was strained and strangled in what she imagined was a high-hat accent that ludicrously overreached itself and plunged the poor woman into farce. Her outward appearance was all effort and contrivance.

Since Lavender had been bought a pony, her mother had been wearing tailored tweed slacks with a matching cap. These items of clothing were bad enough, but then she had acquired the ghastliest little cape, which gave her the look of Sherlock Holmes. To say the very least, it was simply not at all the thing. She was the epitome of a dreaded social climber who was trying to cut a dash with the gentry.

Lavender's Under-12s riding class was scheduled as the third event in the children's classes. She decided to plait Bingle's carefully pulled mane before they left, and fetching her kit from the tack room, she began. She did like to be organised and had carefully laid out all her equipment several days ago. Although most children love to jump and gallop and enter races, Lavender's favourite activity was preparing Bingle for riding classes. She enjoyed the polishing and plaiting and had even recently begun to use one of her old toothbrushes to clean his teeth so that his breath was sweet and minty-fresh for the judges. They were also entered in the Under-12s showjumping, but strangely this did not thrill Lavender half as much as the preparation for the showing events. Perhaps she was destined to be a groom for a showing stable. Can you imagine what Mrs E-H would think of that? A lowly groom!

Her mother came out to chivvy her back into the house to eat breakfast.

"Now, do *not* rub out your plaits while I am away," Lavender instructed Bingle, who looked at her with wise and knowing eyes. He knew what this was all about. With his keen pony intuition, he knew that today was the day of Chatton Show.

Lavender clattered behind her mother back to the modernised manor house. It was an unfortunate combination of the old and the new. Mrs E-H was very keen to be stylish, and she craved the modern conveniences that just did not suit the old style. Sadly, her vision of Gracious Living had gone awry. The small original rooms that had had a charm of their own had been knocked through. Now the living room was like a long rectangle, the shape of a shoe-box, vaguely reminiscent of a toy house designed by an unimaginative child. There were a variety of 'modern' conveniences such as electrically-heated fake logs that replaced the lovely old Inglenook fireplace, a cocktail bar in the very worst of American styles and a huge, ugly television set that dominated the far end of the room. A tightly-upholstered sofa of shiny material sat in front of the television, so uncomfortable that one slid around without ever finding a relaxing position. The lovely old ceiling with bare wood beams had been plastered over to continue with Mrs E-H's vision of what a 'modern' house should look like.

One could almost hear the old house groaning at its uglification. There was a dispirited sense of newly-created dreariness as it sat, surrounded by a garden that was all pretentious concoction. A carefully gravelled drive swept around the manicured lawn that looked so perfect one dare not walk across it. There were impossibly neat flowerbeds with seried rows of flowers that all stood to attention side-by-side. Garden decorations included birdbaths, a sundial and a sheltered nook that looked like a set on the stage of the local amateur dramatic society.

Everywhere one looked, the surroundings seemed strained and tortured. There was no easy sense of shabby comfort. Lavender longed for their old cottage, which had been so friendly and fun, where they had lived before her father's meteoric rise through the ranks of a big insurance company in Oxford. It would be logical that increased wealth should make life happier and easier, but in the case of Mrs E-H, it seemed to become more tortured as if she had to conform to some bizarre version of their new position in society.

However, today was the local horse event of the year, and Lavender had no time to muse on this sad state of affairs. She smiled in a kindly fashion at their maid, Claire, who was dressed in a ridiculous black and white uniform, hovering beside the bowl of corn flakes sitting ready with a milk jug and matching sugar bowl.

"You will never guess what is occurring today," announced Mrs E-H, while Lavender obediently spooned crunchy cereal into her mouth.

"It is Jill Crewe! She is giving a dressage exhibition on that new horse. Apparently, she bought it from some sort of circus. Talk about showing off!"

"But that is so exciting! I'm sure everyone would love to see his performance," said Lavender, who was as kind-hearted as her mother was judgemental. She was a devoted Jill fan.

"Dear Susan is commentating. She was telling me about it last night. She thinks it's rather bad form," said Mrs E-H.

Mrs E-H had been to school with Susan's mother, Mrs Pyke, and they shared a passion for spiky, hot-house flowers that they displayed all around their respective homes. Susan had not advised on the purchase of Bingle. She had been away on holiday with relatives in Torquay at the time. Had she been consulted, she would have firmly rejected the idea. It was only by sheer good luck that Mr E-H's friend from the golf course had told him about a pony for sale, and he had quite uncharacteristically acted on a whim and purchased him immediately.

Lavender kept her eyes on her cereal bowl. She was well aware that there was some ill-feeling between Jill and Susan. It went all the way back to when they had been at school together. She was fond of her Aunt Susan, but equally, she had a great admiration for Jill, who had given her riding lessons. She had read every one of Jill's pony books, from the originals which had starred Black Boy and Rapide to the more recent ones that detailed Jill's adult adventures.

"Is Aunt Susan not riding then? Is she going to give up riding altogether now that she is married?"

"She isn't sure. Her father, dear Georgie, still has the stables. He is happy to mount her so that she can continue with her riding career. But she says that it is something she feels she might have grown out of."

Lavender gave this idea some serious thought. She couldn't imagine ever 'growing out' of her obsession with all things horsey. There were millions of grown-ups in the world who still rode, competing in competitions, hacking, foxhunting and breeding horses. Perhaps, once the novelty of being married had worn off, Aunt Susan would realise that life without horses was rather dull.

"It should be a good day today," said Lavender, trying to change the subject. "I've got my riding class, and then we're entered in the jumping. Bingle should go well. I was rather hoping we might win our first blue ribbon."

"I won't be pleased if you don't," snapped Mrs E-H. "Hopefully, the judges know their business."

"I have a good feeling about today," said Lavender, determined to remain positive, crossing her fingers and hoping that she wasn't going to jinx her chances.

She hated the idea of selling Bingle. It was not just that she couldn't bear to part with him, but if he were sold, as he got older, he was in danger of falling down into a situation such as a disreputable riding school. Lavender just couldn't bear the thought of it. She would have to jump on him and ride off into the wilderness to keep him safe. Much as she disliked their soulless house, she didn't much fancy sleeping in the roots of an old tree in a forest and trying to live off berries and nuts as Dinah Dean had all those years ago.

As Claire cleared away the breakfast things, Lavender hurried upstairs to get changed into her best riding outfit. She had a neat blue coat with a matching blue-velvet riding cap, beige jodhpurs, brown ankle boots, a pale-blue shirt and a navy-blue tie. The night before, she had painstakingly packed all the equipment into the horsebox, and now it was merely a matter of leading Bingle up the ramp, tying him securely and setting off for the showground.

They arrived at eight o'clock, early enough to secure a premium parking spot, under a large, shady tree, not too far from the ringside. The local riders who hacked to the showground were trickling in through the gateway, calling out cheerful greetings to each other. Harassed mothers, driving small cars piled high with buckets of horse feed, boxes of grooming kit and extra riding clothes, were tootling in and driving around looking for good places to park. Everyone seemed to know each other, and Lavender felt very conscious that no one talked to them. Her mother just did not seem to have the knack for making friends, and she must have inherited this unfortunate character trait. She was always so shy, and other children interpreted this as stand-offishness.

Bingle walked down the ramp and looked around. For just a minute, it seemed that he might be searching for something. Perhaps it was his former owner, Jill. Perhaps he sensed that she might already be here. Lavender tied him up beside the horsebox, pulled off his rug and began to brush him. There was at least an hour before her class would be called.

"I'll go and get your number," said Mrs E-H. She trit-trotted across the grass, stepping carefully to avoid droppings.

Lavender pulled out her saddle and her show bridle and tacked up. She polished her boots with a soft rag before she carefully mounted. She would ride Bingle around for a while to warm him up and become accustomed to his surroundings. She loved this moment, the beginning of the show, when everyone's hopes and dreams were shimmering through the air. There was the smell of freshly crushed grass, the crackling of the loudspeaker sending energy around the air, the coloured bunting flapping in the fresh summer breeze paying homage to the great art of horse riding. Fat shiny cattle were parading around the centre ring.

They were about to ride over to the exercise ring for children when Mrs E-H hurried back from the Secretary's tent, flapping the number peevishly.

"Lavender, darling! You must tie this on!"

"It's alright, Mummy. There's plenty of time," she said as quietly as possible. She looked around surreptitiously, hoping that other people wouldn't notice them.

Her mother tied her number around her arm.

"I'm just going to go and ride around in the exercise area. Get Bingle warmed up for his class," said Lavender.

Bingle stepped out, arching his neck, resplendent in his gleaming tack with a neatly plaited mane and tail and a glossy polished black coat.

"Oh! It's Black Boy!" called out a girl, who was perhaps fifteen-years-old on a scrawny skewbald gelding with a hogged mane.

"That's right," said her companion, a thin girl with blond plaits. "He used to belong to Jill Crewe."

Lavender smiled at them shyly. If she had had more confidence, she would have ridden over and chatted, but she was tongue-tied and embarrassed. She trotted onto the exercise arena and joined a large circle of riders who were going around. She was feeling very nervous, much more than normal. What had seemed to be a jolly jaunt to her local show had now turned into a monstrous test of nightmare proportions. If she didn't come first, her mother would sell Bingle. She shuddered at the thought. Her mouth was dry. Looking around at the other riders, she tried to work out which would be in her class. She hardly knew any of the local children who all seemed to be the best of buddies, shouting back and forth at each other, their mothers huddled together in groups around the edge of the arena.

She began to chant to herself good advice, things that she must remember when she got into the ring. 'Don't get caught up in a bunch. Don't let other children on their ponies barge into me. Don't get too close to a pony that might kick in front of me. Keep my hands still and steady, heels down.'

There was so much to remember. The saddle was feeling slippery, and suddenly, she was very insecure, as if she were perched on top of it rather than sitting into it.

"It's funny, Miss Pomfret, the judge today. You know she always chooses chestnut ponies. They say she adores chestnuts and won't look at a black," said one of the girls trotting past on a beautifully turned-out chestnut pony with four white socks and a perfect diamond-shaped star in the exact centre of its broad forehead.

We haven't a hope, thought Lavender, her heart flopping down through her boots. Bingle will be sold. Mummy will insist that I have some horribly bad-tempered, flashy, chestnut mare, just so Miss Pomfret will choose us next time. To her intense humiliation, she felt tears welling in her eyes. She hated this showing business. Parading around trying to be the best. It was the most ridiculous thing she had ever heard of!

Eventually, they called her class into the collecting ring. The brass band had struck up a cheerful tune, and the ponies seemed to be marching in time to the music. Completely at odds with the jolly tune, Lavender felt utterly woebegone. She knew that they would not even get called in. There would be no opportunity to give a show, and her mother would be so disappointed and angry that Bingle would be sent to a horse sale in Rychester within a month.

She looked at the judge, the horrid Miss Pomfret, who was wearing a tweed jacket, cavalry twill breeches, and a jaunty pork-pie hat stuck with feathers and badges. She looked very mannish, and there was a distinct suggestion of a moustache on her upper lip. She did not look like an inspired person who might award Bingle the first rosette to save him from an ignominious dismissal.

Lavender's downcast and desperate mood must have been communicated to Bingle, and he walked with his head hanging low as if he sensed some deep disgrace. He plodded disconsolately. Lavender lifted her hands too high in a desperate effort to raise his head, but as her hands rose, her toes pointed down to the ground.

At the steward's command to trot, Lavender was so flustered and distressed that she was rising on the wrong diagonal, which is a technical fault of the highest magnitude. Then, came the order to canter and she gave Bingle an incorrect aid, and he struck off on the wrong leading leg. After this appalling display, they were sent to the bottom of the back line.

Lavender rode out of the ring, and her mother rushed up to her.

"Lavender! What on earth went wrong?" she shrieked at her.

Lavender cringed. She hated the way her mother always spoke in such a shrill voice, drawing attention to themselves. Lavender felt her face burning. She was puce with embarrassment, wanting to curl up and die.

"It was all my fault," she said. "It wasn't Bingle. It was *my* fault. I have to go back to the horsebox."

She trotted away before there was any opportunity for her mother to continue the harangue.

She dismounted and untacked Bingle and threw his rug over him, making sure he had his haynet and a bucket of clean water. Then she spied her mother and Susan King making their way over.

"Oh, poor Lavender!" exclaimed Susan. "How utterly mortifying to be banished to the bottom of the back row. You know, I think it is down to that pony. No mount of Jill Crewe's is ever going to be any good. I'm going to find you a proper pony, something with some blood, something that will put you in the winner's circle."

At this point, Lavender couldn't find the courage to speak up. Tears were spilling down her face. Finally, she managed to mutter.

"I love him. I love him. I don't care about winning rosettes. I don't see the point."

"Now, don't get hysterical, child," admonished her mother. "Of course, you're upset. Competing at shows and winning is extremely important. You know that!"

"Don't you see, if I can't get called in on Bingle, then a more expensive pony is going to make me look like an utter fool. Like someone who thinks that spending a lot of money on a show pony makes me a better rider than other people."

After this impassioned plea, she ran off. She just couldn't bear it. She hated her mother and Aunt Susan for their wrong-headed attitudes. They didn't seem to have any sort of love for animals themselves. They just saw them as objects that should carry one to glory. She would have loved to talk to Jill. She would understand, not only about loving your pony but about real horsemanship, not this ridiculous charade trying to get rosettes.

In her desperation, Lavender just wanted to be alone. She found herself amongst the crowd that was watching the adult classes. Jill would be here somewhere, but she didn't have the courage to find her and talk to her. She knew that she would sound like a pathetic idiot.

There was a hack class in the main ring, and she fixed her eyes on the circling horses but didn't really take it in. She knew, at the very least, she should be taking note of the way in which the winning horses went, picking up some pointers for successful ringcraft, but she didn't have any hope left in her.

She had to think of a plan. A way to persuade her mother that Bingle was her beloved friend, not just an accessory to be used to show off. In desperation she considered talking to her father. It was the only thing she could think of.

Chapter Two – Stay of Execution

Aunt Susan's voice was floating over the loudspeaker. She was talking about Jill Crewe and Skydiver. Lavender turned her head with the rest of the people around her and saw Jill floating in wearing the most sumptuous outfit, a long riding coat and a top hat and Skydiver lifting his hoofs like a dancer, floating over the ground and around the outside of the arena. This must be the dressage exhibition.

Lavender was glad of a distraction. She watched Jill and Skydiver go through their routine and felt inspired. She wished that one day she might be able to ride like that. Then a strange noise came over the loudspeaker, and she could feel ripples of laughter running through the crowd around her.

"Oh, Barty!" crackled Aunt Susan's voice. "You are naughty. Oh! That tickles!"

An old man in a tweed coat began to run towards the wooden box that stood on stilts from where the commentary came. The spectators tittered and pointed. The loudspeaker was turned off. Jill bowed to the crowd and exited the arena. There was a splatter of applause from the crowd. Lavender joined in as loudly as she could. This was awful for Jill, but also for Aunt Susan. How humiliating!

Jill's voice was loud and indignant, talking to someone at the entrance of the ring.

"Susan ruined it with her stupid carry-on. What was that about?"

Lavender walked back to the horsebox. Her mother was there flapping around.

"Oh! Poor Susan! I can't believe that that husband did this to her! The humiliation of it all!"

She was wringing her hands in anguish.

"It's not that bad," said Lavender. Being a kind-hearted girl, she was trying to soothe her mother's upset feelings.

"Lavender!" said Mrs E-H. "You must get ready. Where on earth did you get to? It's your jumping class. I can hear it being called."

Lavender was truly flustered now. She had forgotten all about the showjumping, so sunk in misery over her failure in the riding class. She threw on her saddle and pulled up the girth. Her mother dashed around, getting in the way rather than helping. Then she was cantering over to the ring. There wouldn't even be time to walk the course. She hated it when she had to rush. She liked to be organised all the time.

Serena, the riding instructor from Mrs Darcy's riding school, was in the collecting ring, checking stirrup lengths and tightening girths for the students that were entered.

"Violet! Remember, don't look down as you go over the jump. Head up!" she said to the young girl riding Blackstone.

"Oh! Hello Lavender! Of course, you've entered too. Good luck! I'm sure you'll ride well."

Somehow this cheered up Lavender hugely. She took heart. Onward and upward. Bingle deserved her best effort. It wasn't his fault that she had failed miserably in the riding class this morning. Nor was it the end of the world!

There were still a few competitors walking the course.

"Would you mind holding Bingle's reins while I walk around the jumps?" she asked Serena.

"Of course, darling. Quick! Run in! There's not much time. I can talk you through it afterwards," said Serena.

Lavender sprinted around the jumps. They were all in logical order and not particularly high. There was nothing here that she hadn't jumped before. She got back to the collecting ring, and Serena gave herself, Violet and another little boy called Tom some last-minute words of advice.

"There should be five strides between the second jump and on that left-hand curve around to the third. Remember to try and land on the left leading leg, and it might help to count out loud, so you get it right."

Lavender's spirits lifted. This was the sort of help that she needed, not her mother and Aunt Susan's waspish comments on the other competitors. Violet and Blackstone were called into the ring before her. She watched carefully. Little Blackstone was an old hand at this type of competition. He cantered smartly up to the first jump, a brush fence, popped over it, and set off determinedly for the next fence. Violet looked nervous, but she was trying her best. They would have gone clear, but just as they were to jump the last fence, a plastic bag dropped by a careless person in the crowd of spectators floated across in front of them. Blackstone shied a little and ran out. Violet came out, her eyes filled with tears, her mouth turned down in disappointment.

"Sweetheart, don't be upset. You did a great job. It really wasn't your fault. Just one of those things," said Serena soothingly.

"Oh well done!" said Lavender. "I'm sure I would have fallen off if it had happened to me!"

Violet smiled weakly. It suddenly occurred to Lavender how pleasant it was to have people to talk to. She wondered if her mother might let her go to the riding school for her lessons in the future, rather than having private lessons at home. It would be great fun to have some friends who rode ponies. If she went to the local school, then she might be chums with some of the neighbourhood children who rode, but her mother insisted that she attend a small, exclusive school in Birtle, twenty miles from Chatton, in the opposite direction to Rychester. None of the girls rode, and Lavender had no opportunity to read gymkhana schedules and discuss which classes they were to enter, followed by Monday morning inquests on what happened and who had won what. At school, Lavender found herself, as usual, the outsider.

Her number was called, and she rode into the ring. To pay homage to the gods she did a couple of flying changes as she cantered over to the judges. She saluted and circled until the bell rang. Then she was flying through the start, feeling as if she were on Pegasus. They cleared every jump and galloped the last few strides through the finish. She heard applause from the spectators.

"Oh! Well done Lavender!" called Serena.

"Wow!" said Violet.

"It was just a fluke," Lavender said modestly.

"There's been three other clear rounds, so far. You're going to have to jump off."

She had been floating on a cloud of determination, and now she plummeted to earth. Nervousness overtook her. In the jump-off there were four jumps, and somehow they managed to hit every single one of them. She was fourth. There wasn't even a rosette. Her mother was at the ringside with a pinched, ugly face.

Lavender was empty with fear, aching through a void of disappointment. She would be forced to sell Bingle. She would lose him. Then, it came to her. She would enter the Under-14s, and she would jump to the stars, just to prove that Bingle was a pony to be celebrated.

Her mother went and made her entry. Then she asked Serena if she might walk the course with her and the two riding school students who were entering.

"You did so well in the first round," said Serena.

"But then I lost it all," she said plaintively, in a small voice.

"This is your first real competition. It takes years of experience to maintain a top performance in every round," said Serena. "Don't be so hard on yourself!"

"But if I don't win, Mummy is going to sell Bingle," moaned Lavender. Just saying the words out loud made this awful truth real.

"Oh," said Serena, looking shocked. She was at a loss. "Do you think I could talk to her? Tell her how Bingle is a very good pony for your current stage?"

"I don't think that will help," said Lavender. "Unless you were a member of the local aristocracy."

"I guess that's not me," said Serena, whose father was a bus driver. "But I will help you with some advice."

Lavender focused determinedly on the jumps. The course was quite similar to the Under-12s but a good six inches higher and with the addition of a water jump, which was new to Chatton Show. A new sponsor, Triangle Tractors, had proudly financed it, and their name was emblazoned on the bottom of the water tray. The black letters lurked below the glittering water and made it even more strange and scary for the ponies.

"I've never jumped water," said Lavender helplessly.

"No, but I'm sure Bingle has," said Serena, "just ride him quite fast at it, as if it were a wide obstacle."

There were more than twenty competitors, only a handful of those that had also jumped in the Under-12s. As Lavender had entered at the last moment, she was the last competitor to jump. She dismounted and, holding Bingle on the edge of the ring, she watched each competitor. She counted strides between fences, looked at angles, and in particular paid attention to how they jumped the water jump.

There were four clear rounds when it was her turn to go. She channelled every ounce of her being into getting it exactly right. There was no showing-off with flying changes as she approached the judges at a sober trot. Bingle seemed to understand how important this competition was, and he trotted carefully, each hoof placed on the ground neatly and rhythmically.

The bell rang and they cantered in a wide half-circle, through the start, and straight to the first jump - an easy brush. Bingle popped over it like an old hand and cantered steadily onto a post-and-rails. Lavender counted the strides in her head, and her pony took off in exactly the right place. Up and over clear. Then, on to the triple. Lavender urged him on at a faster pace. Bingle lengthened his stride, and as he jumped, he stretched his neck out, and Lavender pushed her hands forward to make sure she didn't jab him in the mouth. As they landed, she turned him to the right, and maintaining a fast pace; they headed for the wide water jump. The surface glinted in the sunlight, and Lavender forced herself to feel determined, not to give Bingle a moment to hesitate and imagine that the black lettering beneath the water was a bunch of marauding sharks. The thought didn't occur to her that Bingle would have no knowledge of sharks. He jumped high and wide, and she felt herself slip sideways above the saddle. But the faithful, kind Bingle landed and seemed to pause to give her a moment to regain her balance, and they went on towards the double. There were no tricky distances between the two fences, and they popped the first one, two regular strides and clear over the next. Then, they turned right and headed for the imposing red brick wall. Bingle shook his head as if to tell his rider that this was no problem. He'd been jumping walls all his life. Up and over and then, they headed towards the last fence. Lavender didn't allow herself to lose her concentration. She had watched at least two other competitors who had gone clear until the last fence, and become careless, they had brought down the top pole.

"A clear round for Lavender Ellison-Heath and Bingle Jells," announced the loudspeaker. "There will be five competitors to jump off."

Lavender trotted out of the ring, patting Bingle effusively and telling him he was the best pony in the whole world.

"Oh! Well done!" shouted Serena.

Violet ran up to Bingle and gave him a piece of apple as a reward, stroking his soft velvety nose and whispering congratulations. Lavender bent forward, buried her face in his plaited mane, and put her arms around his neck.

The jump-off was announced, five jumps and Lavender was drawn to go last, lucky last. This gave her the advantage of knowing how the other competitors went. If none of them were clear, she would have all the time in the world to go slow and as long as she hit nothing, nor refused, she would win. If the others went clear, then she would have some idea of just how fast she had to push to beat their times.

Her mother scurried over.

"Oh! Lavender! You absolutely must do well in the jump-off after that abysmal attempt in the last competition!" she screeched.

Lavender cringed, but her mother didn't seem to notice.

"I have to look and memorise the order of the five jumps in the jump-off," she said and rode off to the other side of the collecting ring to stand near the ringside. She was relieved to see that the water jump was not included, but the wall had another layer of bricks added to it.

The other competitors all looked older mounted on larger ponies than Bingle, who was only 13.2 hh. The first girl on a skinny bay mare looked at least sixteen-years-old. Lavender didn't believe she could possibly be under fourteen. Her mare was unhappy, with rolling white eyes, swishing her tail from side to side. But they jumped clear and fast, and Lavender knew she was going to be hard to beat. She began to wonder if she might just aim for a reasonably fast but clear round. The next three competitors scorched around at the speed of light, and each had at least one fence down. Lavender knew that if she jumped a slow clear, then she was assured second place. Would that be enough to appease her mother?

She knew that she had to decide, and she was wavering between trying to win at top speed or being careful and going clear in order to get second. The bell rang, and they flashed through the start. Bingle seemed to understand that this was a jump-off and speed was important, and he cantered smartly towards the first fence, landed and put on a spurt.

"You think we should go fast," said Lavender, taking her cue from him, and she leaned forward and guided him but let him choose his own pace. It seemed that he had taken charge, and she acknowledged that he had been in far more jumping competitions than herself. They zoomed around, and there were no sounds of poles clattering. They had gone clear. It had to be close. The voice over the loudspeaker announced her time. It was one second faster than the girl on the skinny bay mare. They had won! It was not only a blue ribbon but a rather impressive silver cup. She laughed as they cantered around the ring. She felt as if it should be the final chapter of a pony book, as had been Jill and Black Boy's win at the end of *Jill's Gymkhana,* but there were many more exciting events to follow before the end of this story.

Chapter Three – Meeting Ruby Swope

"Lavender, you did frightfully well with Bingle at the show," said Mrs E-H on the following morning. "Perhaps I was too quick to write him off."

Lavender felt an enormous weight roll from her shoulders. She had been so afraid that her beloved Bingle was to be sacrificed for the galloping social ambitions of her mother. Now, at least, she had a stay of execution.

"I thought perhaps we might take him to a bigger event. A competition that would really mean something, not just a local show."

Lavender looked at her in horror. It was as if any wins they scored would only set the bar higher, and there would be more pressure on them.

"I thought I might talk to Susan and see if she has any ideas. You know an event that would be a fitting finale to this summer. Next season you will be twelve-years-old, so you'll be competing in the Under-14s regularly, and perhaps also the Under-16s. But obviously, you're both up to it."

Lavender saw then that she had cornered herself. No matter how well they performed, it would merely feed her mother's desperate desire to prove herself to the world. If only there were another arena in which she could achieve whatever ineffable prize her mother was seeking.

"I'm going to put Bingle out in the field today. He deserves a day off," she said, excusing herself from the table and getting up.

"Don't forget, we've got church at eleven o'clock. Your father will attend with us today."

Lavender didn't mind going to church. She rather liked the atmosphere and the smell of beeswax that had been rubbed lovingly into the wooden pews. She let Bingle go in the field and he sniffed the air. She wished, again, that he had a pony companion. He always looked as if he were searching for a missing friend, perhaps Rapide, the other pony that Jill had owned.

She went inside and put on her grey dress with the neat Peter Pan white collar and buttons sewn down the front. She brushed out her long brown hair and carefully plaited it, tying the ends with white ribbons that matched her dress collar. She stared at herself critically in the mirror. Often people commented on her black eyes that tilted at the edges. Her mother described them as cats' eyes, it made her look vaguely exotic as if she had some foreign blood. Idly, she wondered if perhaps she was adopted. It was not a horrific thought. It would make sense of how her mother and herself were so different in their thoughts and feelings. It would also explain the way she felt so remote and distanced from her father. He was vaguely affectionate, but she never felt any real connection to him. Perhaps, that was why she was so desperate to hang on to Bingle. He was the closest thing she had to a living being to which she felt a deep and meaningful bond.

Susan and Barty King attended church, and Lavender saw her mother in a huddle with them. They were probably discussing the showjumping career that was being thrust upon her.

"Lavender, darling," said Susan, who had recently changed the way she spoke. She had adopted a gushing style, punctuated with breathless pauses. "I was thinking you absolutely must go to Chesterton Show. It is a rather important County show, with two days of showjumping. Daddy insisted that I go there when I was jumping when I was still at school. I was thinking I should come over and give you some coaching. You've got a week to practise."

Lavender stretched her mouth in a fixed, tight-lipped smile. Until now, she had been taught first by Jill, then by Serena. Aunt Susan had come over and inspected the new arena and watched her cantering some circles, but she had avoided being instructed by her. She loved her aunt, but she was aware of the tension between Jill and Susan, and she wasn't looking forward to another instructor. Especially when it seemed from Jill's books that Susan's riding style left lots to be desired.

"I would appreciate that," she replied politely. "I'll write and ask the secretary for a schedule."

She knew that her attendance at Chesterton was inevitable. The huge effort she had made yesterday in order to win the Under-14s was going to have to be repeated, and they would have to get over bigger jumps and beat much better riders. It was the only way for her to keep Bingle.

"Could I perhaps go to Mrs Darcy's and have some riding lessons there, rather than Serena coming to our place. I think it would be good for me to get used to riding in different places if I'm to be going from one show to another," she said politely to her mother on the way home.

"Yes, you're quite right. You're ready to face the hurly-burly, and it will be good for you to be rubbing shoulders with other riders, even if they are only the bottom rung of local riders who don't even own their own ponies" said Mrs E-H.

On Tuesday, Lavender gave Bingle an extra special grooming until he was shining, oiled his hoofs, tacked up and tied him to the ring in the stable wall. Then, she went inside and up to her bedroom and pulled on her second-best jodhpurs, buttoned up a white shirt and carefully knotted her yellow tie.

They trotted down the road to the riding school. She was to join the ten o'clock lesson. Serena had told her that Violet was in this lesson and she was rather hoping that she and Violet might become friends. To children who enjoyed a more normal life, thrown into the throng of other young people with brothers and sisters, truckloads of friends and sparring partners this might have seemed a strange desire. To Lavender, it was a hopeless aspiration. She had read in her Noel and Henry pony books by Josephine Pullein-Thompson about the pony club where children chattered, argued, exchanged banter and indulged in throwing wet sponges at each other in the tack room and it all seemed like an impossible dream.

It was a small class, including two other pupils riding their own ponies. Violet was there mounted on Blackstone and she smiled in a friendly fashion at Lavender. A girl with frizzy gold hair sticking out around the edges of her velvet cap riding a washed-out palomino looked at Lavender with pale blue eyes.

"Hello," said Lavender timidly, unnerved by the girl's stare.

The girl looked blank. Lavender thought she was rather like a loopy Christmas tree angel.

"Angela is riding her own pony, Christie," said Violet confidentially. "Don't worry. She never talks to anyone. Dougie, over there on that gorgeous grey, he's got his own pony as well. Isn't it beautiful?"

Lavender looked over. Obviously, Violet was referring to the pony, not Dougie himself, who had a huge nose with wide-blown nostrils and decorated with a splattering of pancake freckles. The grey was certainly eye-catching, perhaps a Welsh pony with a big dollop of Arab blood, stepping delicately with its neck arched and its tail carried like a banner.

They trotted a circle in the arena, and then Serena told them to shorten their stirrups to a length suitable for jumping. The grid was set up; a row of twelve cavallettis at eighteen inches in height.

"First, I want you to knot your reins and then down the grid once, around and down again. The second time you drop your reins and cross your arms in front of your chest" commanded Serena.

Lavender suppressed a cry of alarm. This was exactly the sort of thing that they did in books. She even remembered having seen a photo of cavalry officers jumping bareback carrying saddles on their arms. Perhaps that would be the next instruction. She couldn't imagine riding bareback and carrying her saddle hanging over her arm. Surely you would have to be superhuman to manage that manoeuvre.

All the students carried out the instructions, and Lavender thanked her lucky stars that Bingle was such a kind and reliable old chap. He must have been through activities like this a hundred times in his life. He was not at all fazed. Lavender found that she enjoyed the bouncing feeling; the speed and the rhythm were exciting.

"Now, I want you to cross your stirrups and we'll do some circles at the rising trot," said Serena.

This was a challenge, but certainly, a good exercise thought Lavender. Undoubtedly, next, they would be jumping down the grid with no stirrups. This was the case. Then one of the little boys, Ted, a chap with bright red hair and large freckles across his snub nose, fell off. The dun pony, Mousie, stopped and turned around and nudged him with her nose. Obviously, students falling off was an everyday occurrence for her.

Everyone pulled up to watch and saw, to their relief Ted leap to his feet, calling, "I'm alright, I'm alright," and scrambled back into the saddle. It struck Lavender then that she had never fallen off in her life. Bingle had always looked after her so well. If she even felt unbalanced, he seemed to move beneath her in the right direction for her to remain in the saddle. She knew that sooner or later, as a young horsewoman, she was going to have her first fall. She hoped that it wasn't going to be at Chesterton Show next Saturday!

After the lesson, they all rode back to the stable yard. A skinny little girl with dark skin and dirty clothes dashed forward and grabbed Bingle's reins.

"What are you doing?" asked Lavender in surprise.

"I'll look after 'im," she squeaked.

"No Ruby, it's alright. That's not one of the riding school ponies. He belongs to Lavender."

" 'e is beautiful," said Ruby, letting go of the reins and stepping back.

"He is rather handsome," agreed Lavender.

"Lavender meet Ruby. She's been helping out at the school lately, in exchange for riding lessons. She's one of my best helpers," said Serena.

"How do you do?" said Lavender. She looked at the girl, thinking she seemed rather underfed. She had a *gamine* quality, with a dark-skinned elfin face.

"Orright," replied the girl.

"His name is Bingle," said Lavender, dismounting. She recognised a kindred spirit, another person who loved Bingle.

"Would you like a ride?" asked Lavender.

"Surely I do," replied Ruby.

Lavender smiled at the girl's accent. It was everything that her mother would hate. Offering her a ride on Bingle was a small act of rebellion against her mother's ridiculous pretensions.

"You can go down the bottom field. There's no ponies in there," said Serena, beaming approval at the two of them. On the quiet, Serena was a bit of a 'do-gooder'. She believed that putting certain people together would be good for both of them, and Lavender and Ruby were both in need of help in entirely different ways. Ruby was tough and determined but lived in difficult family circumstances in poverty. In contrast, Lavender was sweet, and entitled but seemed lost and friendless.

Ruby adjusted the stirrup leathers, and they had to be put on the shortest hole. She scrambled aboard and picked up the reins. Lavender went ahead and opened the gate. Bingle walked into the field, and Ruby was soon trotting around, a huge grin spread across her little pixie face.

"'e's dreamy!" she called.

"Yes, he's the best pony in the world," agreed Lavender.

"Can 'e jump?" asked Ruby.

"He can," said Lavender.

"Can I canta 'im?" asked Ruby.

"Of course, a couple of times around the field, then he's probably had enough for the day," said Lavender.

Ruby was a natural rider. She sat in the saddle as if she were born there. Although her leg position was a little too far forward and her arms straight, as if she were pushing a pram, she had a fantastic seat. The arrangement of arms and legs could be altered, but the way one sits in the saddle, a good 'seat' is a gift from the gods.

"How long have you been riding?" asked Lavender when Ruby came back over to her.

"I always wanted ta ride. 'ere and there I get rides. Serena be good, she 'elps me."

"You work here at the riding school, then?" asked Lavender.

"Thas right. I'm 'ere ev'ry day."

"You can ride Bingle again tomorrow if you want. I'll bring him up for you. What time is best?" asked Lavender.

"Oh! Wow!" cried Ruby.

"Lunchtime be best, 'bout one."

"I'll come up tomorrow then," said Lavender. "I'll get my mother to book me another lesson tomorrow morning. I've got to go to this show at Chesterton, on Saturday. So, I need to practise."

"You be so lucky!" sighed Ruby.

"I guess I am," said Lavender. Looking at it from Ruby's point of view, she could see how it looked. She was a rich kid with her own pony being taken around the shows. If it were only that simple!

The next day Serena gave Lavender a private lesson, and Ruby was on hand to do the jumps.

"What is it that you need help with?" asked Serena.

"I think it's the whole thing. Like I jump my jumps at home, but when it comes to a complete course, I find it hard to concentrate."

"Yes, I guess that sort of thing comes from experience. You need to practise in competitions, and you'll improve."

"But I don't have time!" cried Lavender.

"What's the hurry? You're only eleven. You've got years in children's classes ahead of you. This is your first season, and you won the Under-14 class at Chatton Show. You're doing great!" said Serena.

"Tell that to my mother," said Lavender pitifully, tears running down her face.

"Oh, sweetheart. You mustn't cry. Is your mother very ambitious for you?" asked Serena.

"She keeps wanting to trade Bingle in on something fancy, more expensive, more showy. I'm just desperate to keep Bingle, I love him so much. He is my heart horse!"

"But that be orrful!" cried Ruby, on the side lines.

"I can talk to your mother, if you like?" offered Serena. "I do think that Bingle is just perfect for you right now."

At this point the lesson dissolved into Lavender crying helplessly. Serena tried to comfort her. Ruby stood by watching in horror.

Lavender woke on the morning of the big show with a feeling of doom. Everything today was going to end in disaster, she could feel it in her bones. Usually, she managed a cheerful and obedient demeanour with her mother, but today she was sullen. Mrs E-H didn't seem to notice. She was running high on dreams of huge success that would lead her to a celebrated position at the heights of the gymkhana social scene.

The sky was an unusual pale lemon and grey with tiny dark-purple clouds massing on the horizon. Summer was waning with a fresh, sharp breeze. "The winds of change," muttered Lavender to herself and shivered. She had no confidence in her ability to achieve one clear round, let alone dashing around in a jump-off with the fastest winning time. She hated this having to go out and try to win. She wanted to leap onto Bingle's back and ride away to some fairytale land of sunshine, butterflies and warm breezes and live in splendid isolation.

The journey to Chesterton took about an hour. Lavender sat in the front passenger seat, looking out at the flashing fields. She had not bothered to plait Bingle's mane this morning. She had no pleasure in this excursion. At least, she could grab his mane and hang on if she felt insecure going over the huge jumps.

They arrived at the showground, and it was indeed a large event. There were three rings and rows and rows of horseboxes and trailers.

"I'll go over and talk to the secretary," said Mrs E-H. Her voice was more than usually shrill when she was excited. She trit-trotted away in her high heels that mismatched with the tweedy country outfit. Lavender suddenly felt old. Watching her mother, she was cringing with embarrassment, realising just how ridiculous she looked. Bingle pushed at her gently as if to tell her that everything would be alright. He would make it right for her. He wasn't going to leave her.

The first jumping class was the Under-12s competition. Lavender tacked up Bingle and left him tied to the truck while she went over to look at the course. The turf was beautiful, a thick, springy, green velvet, and the jumps were all freshly painted. The course was perfect, well set out with good distances between the jumps, and if only there wasn't the black cloud of losing Bingle hanging over her, then it would be one of those perfect gymkhana days. Lavender felt helpless. Even if they won, if they jumped clear round after clear round, every time, her mother would expect more, and nothing would guarantee that Bingle wouldn't be sold in the future.

She walked back to mount, ignoring her mother's fussing.

"Oh, Lavender, you haven't done his usual hair-do?" Mrs E-H twittered.

"It's not necessary for a jumping class," snapped Lavender.

She and Bingle trotted on ahead to the exercise area and began to warm up in circles. After about twenty minutes, she pulled up her stirrup leathers and jumped the practice jump a few times.

"All competitors for the Under-12s jumping to walk the course!"

Lavender now regretted leaving her mother behind. She needed someone to hold Bingle while she walked the course. Other children were sliding off their ponies and handing the reins over to helpers. Breathless with panic, desperate to walk the course, she knew that she would never get around if she didn't. She rode back out searching for her mother and finally saw her standing alone and forlorn near the ringside.

"Mummy! Mummy!" shouted Lavender, feeling guilty and relieved at the same time. "You need to hold Bingle while I walk the course. I'm sorry I rode off without you."

Her mother took the reins hesitantly and held them at arms' length. Lavender went in and stumbled around the course, counting out strides, imitating the other children who all seemed so self-confident and assured. She went back to the collecting ring and mounted.

"Hey, that's Black Boy, you won the Under-14s at Chatton last week," said a thin girl on a funny little pony with very short legs and a large head, who determinedly reefed the reins through his rider's hands as he put his head down to graze on the delectable juicy grass, not yet crushed by hundreds of iron horseshoes.

"Yes, that's right," said Lavender, flashing her a shy smile.

For just a moment, she felt like a local star, to be recognised for her last win. She looked around for any familiar faces, but there was no one here from Mrs Darcy's riding school. Although, there was a boy who looked familiar. She remembered him from Chatton. He was one of the few riders who had two mounts in the same competition. His father was standing by him, a big pot-bellied man with a red face and fleshy determined nose.

The first rider was called in. A red-headed girl with buck teeth, who rode with great flourish and legs whirling like windmills on a fat, round grey. The gelding ground to a determined halt in front of the first jump, and she tipped over his head and landed in the middle of the brush jump. The obstinate pony put his head down and cropped the grass. People were quietly tittering at this amusing incident. Stewards ran in to help the wailing girl to her feet and led the pony away.

"They're out," said Mrs E-H smugly.

"Shhhh, Mummy. You can't be seen to be unsporting," hissed Lavender.

"I was only saying," said her mother in a high shrill voice that seemed to echo around the ring. Lavender saw several heads turn in their direction.

The next competitor was a girl with long blond plaits who rode a flashy chestnut gelding. Her pony was mincing along in a crab-wise prancing movement, tossing its head and rolling its eyes. She jerked at the reins and kicked him in the ribs. They barrelled around the course very fast, and it was almost a clear round until they dislodged a brick off the wall.

"Four faults," said the commentator over the loudspeaker.

Three more competitors and not one clear round. Lavender and Bingle were next. They cantered into the ring. Bingle gave a proud swish of his tail and shook his head as if to say, 'just leave this to me.'

They cantered over the first brush jump and across the arena to an upright painted bright red and blue. Then left and towards the double. Lavender was getting into it. She forgot about her mother and the desperate need to win. Feeling Bingle's rhythm and enthusiasm, she knew that he enjoyed jumping. She looked towards the next jump, a double with a short stride between the elements, pop, pop, and then turning for the red brick wall, they soared over gloriously, clearing it by several inches.

"A clear round for Lavender Ellison-Heath on Bingle Jells," said the loudspeaker.

She saw her mother jumping up and down, squawking. For once, she didn't care about being embarrassed. She experienced that particular rush of joy known to showjumpers when they achieve a clear round. Bingle had done it for her!

There were ten clear rounds in the competition, so the jump-off was going to be exciting. Never had the results of an Under-12s showjumping competition been so important!

Lavender was able to watch three other competitors do the jump-off before she was called. They all tore around at the speed of light, and each had two jumps down, which probably put them out of the running. She noticed that as they galloped at the jumps, their ponies flattened and dragged off poles with their hind hoofs. It was a matter of juggling speed against accuracy. She decided that rather than speed, she would try to cut corners.

They galloped into the ring and over the first brush jump at a great pace, and then she leaned back and brought Bingle together and placed him to the left of the next jump, ready to land and turn sharp right towards the third.

She misjudged it. As they jumped the blue jump painted with yellow stars, it seemed to collapse beneath them, all the poles clattering to the ground. Shocked and confused, she couldn't think what had happened. Perhaps an earth tremor? Completely flustered, they cantered on and she was able to pull herself together sufficiently to complete the course but without any flourish or determination. It was four faults with an abysmally slow time.

Her mother was outside the ring, wringing her hands in anguish, her mauve-painted talons flashing in the sunshine.

"What happened?" asked Lavender, looking back into the ring to see the helpers completely reconstructing the second jump.

"I don't know. I'm going to protest. The jump just collapsed. It must be the way that it was built."

"No! No! Don't you understand? You don't do things like that! Why can't you behave properly?" hissed Lavender. It was the first time she had openly criticised her mother's behaviour.

Mrs E-H stared at her daughter as if she had been transformed into a snake.

"Lavender!" she squeaked, clearly rattled.

"That was bad luck!" said a tall girl standing close by.

"But what happened?" asked Lavender.

"You were too close to the wing. Your foot touched it. You brought down the fence, not the pony," the girl said, smiling at her.

"Oh," said Lavender, making a mental note, 'don't get too close to the wing'.

"Did you hear that, Mummy? It was my foot hitting the wing. It wasn't Bingle's fault."

Mrs E-H stared at her daughter uncomprehendingly.

"The wing?" she queried.

"You know, the end of the jump, where the poles are attached," replied Lavender impatiently.

"Don't take that tone with me, young lady," retorted her mother.

"I'm taking Bingle back to the horsebox, give him a rest before the next event," said Lavender and rode off.

She had to calm down. Not only the stress of the competition, the fear of losing Bingle and now she found herself backchatting her mother. She wished her father had come. He was a sensible and sober man, not good fun like some fathers, but at least logical and not beset with a snob complex.

After the winners of the Under-12s had gone in to be presented with their rosettes, the loudspeaker was calling competitors to walk the Under-14s course. Lavender took a deep breath and set off, leaving Bingle tied to the truck. He was still saddled, but she had taken off his bridle and loosened his girth. The course was very similar to the Under-12s, obviously higher and a rather tricky double with the pacing either two very long strides or three short strides between the two elements. Lavender paced backwards and forwards trying to decide whether to aim for two or three strides. She stood there listening to other competitors discussing it. She had never attempted such a thing before. Some of the children declared they would push on to two long strides. Others said they would go for three very short strides.

Lavender sprinted back to the horsebox, desperately hoping she wouldn't have a distracting encounter with her mother. If only she had more brothers and sisters, then her mother could have spread her attention over all of them.

She tightened the girth and slipped on the bridle, donned her cap and mounted ready to go. Bingle was his usual sane, sensible self. They trotted towards the collecting ring. The steward called them, and they rode in, saluted the judges and began to canter in a circle, waiting for the bell.

"Not too close to the wings," she chanted under her breath. Just one more thing to remember. They set off, through the start, and cantering confidently and over the brush fence. As they approached the double she decided to leave it to Bingle, he would know what to do. His head was high, his ears pricked. They landed over the first jump and two long strides and over the second part of the double.

"Brilliant boy," muttered Lavender, thinking how clever he was. Then they were heading for the wall and everything felt great. "We're going to do this," muttered Lavender under her breath.

They were cantering back in the direction of the entrance of the ring towards an upright when suddenly the sane and sensible Bingle threw up his head and seemed to be cantering on the spot. He was looking over to the collecting ring and neighed. A loud ringing noise that reverberated around the arena. Lavender was so shocked that she barely had time to try and push him forward towards the next jump when suddenly he began to gallop, head high, over the jump carelessly, bringing down the top pole and straight as an arrow towards the exit.

Lavender lost both stirrups but managed to stay in the saddle, one hand desperately gripping the pommel. Her mouth was agape in astonishment.

She made a feeble attempt to steer him back onto the course, but he forged on relentlessly out of the ring. They plunged through the ponies and riders that were waiting in a group near the entrance, and then Bingle stopped short. At that point, Lavender fell off. She toppled to the ground. It was her first fall. She leapt up unhurt.

Bingle was standing beside her, nuzzling a bay pony. It was about one hand higher than himself, and sitting on top was a young girl who looked as shocked as Lavender felt.

"Oh, look!" shrieked another rider. "It's Black Boy and Rapide back together again."

Then it dawned on Lavender. This was Bingle's best friend, Jill Crewe's other pony.

"Hi, I'm Lavender, and I think your pony must be Rapide," she said to the rider.

"Of course! I've read the books so they must love each other. You didn't get to finish your round!" said the girl.

"No, I didn't."

"I'm Morgan, that is Morgan Pevensy. I've only just inherited Rapide from my sister Porsche."

"They sure love each other," said Lavender.

"I don't think we should ever part them after that dramatic reunion. I'm meant to be jumping soon. I doubt if I could persuade Rapide to go into the ring. You know this pony is famous for having a mind of his own."

"I've read the books too, religiously, and I know he pulls funny faces," said Lavender.

The two girls began to laugh. The situation had suddenly become hilariously funny. Morgan was skinny, freckled, with long, narrow green eyes. Her legs were stick-thin, and there was a gap between the top of her boots and the bottom of her jodhpur legs.

"Lavender!" called her mother, in her high shrill voice.

"Oh, no," groaned Lavender.

"What on earth happened? I knew that pony was no good. He just carted you out of the ring. He's got to go. We'll get you a decent animal."

These words struck a chill in Lavender's heart. She wanted the ground to open up so she could sink down through a crack and not ever surface again. Never had she felt more embarrassed by her mother.

"Hello!" called Morgan. "This is Rapide. He is Black Boy's best friend."

Mrs E-H stared at her with a crease between her forehead.

"What are you talking about, you silly girl?" she snapped. "And that pony, he is pulling the most ferocious of faces at me, as if I were a monster."

"Oh, hello. What's happened here?" asked a woman hurrying up. She was older, late forties, her long brown hair bundled up in a messy bun; her saggy grey cardigan hung from thin shoulders; flared black trousers flapped around her legs.

Mrs E-H looked her over critically. What a down-trodden mess!

"Oh, Mummy. It was amazing. Black Boy has found Rapide. Look at them! Aren't they sweet!" said Morgan.

"Oh, you clever boys!" said the woman, rubbing both their noses.

"Excuse me," said Mrs E-H in her most hoity-toity voice. "I don't think it's clever at all."

"I'm sorry. Let me introduce myself. I'm Aggie Pevensy, this is my daughter Morgan and I guess Rapide needs no introduction."

Mrs E-H wrinkled her nostrils with disapproval. These people had high hat accents, but it must be just for show. The girl wore ill-fitting jodhpurs, and her appalling mother dressed in rags. Obviously, not at all the type of people with whom she wished to be associated.

"Lavender! Come! Back to the horsebox!"

"I don't want them to be separated!" cried Lavender. "They've only just found each other!"

"I'm not sure that Morgan is going to be able to persuade Rapide to go into the ring. She's not the keenest jumper in the world, and this pony is a character. He knows his own mind," said Aggie Pevensy.

"Why don't I come with you?" suggested Morgan to Lavender. "So, they can stay together for a while. Mummy, I really don't want to jump anyway."

"Alright darling. I think that this time you can get out of it," sighed Aggie. "I'll tell the steward that you won't be competing."

Rapide and Black Boy, now called Bingle, walked together. Morgan and Lavender were chattering away. Mrs E-H walked behind, stiff with

disapproval. She had no intention of allowing Lavender to be friends with this socially undesirable girl.

"Why did you change his name?" asked Morgan.

"It was strange. I just liked the idea of Bingle Jells. Like kind of a joke. Do you think I should change it back?" asked Lavender.

"I don't know. I don't suppose he really cares. I've only just got Rapide. My sister, Porsche, had him before me, but she's turned sixteen, and she's determined to ride in adult classes on proper horses. No more ponies for her. She's demanding that Mercedes share her competition horses with her."

"Who is Mercedes?" asked Lavender. It struck her now. They all had car names.

"She's my older, older sister. She's twenty. The most fabulous rider. She does eventing and also showjumping. She's set for great things, so they say in the equestrian world, also a great beauty."

"You've all got automotive names," said Lavender.

"I know. It's so weird. There's my eldest brother, Royce, then Mercedes, then my other brother Austin, and then Porsche and me. I'm the youngest. They all ride horses, and they're all great riders, except me. I don't mind riding a bit, but there's no way I want to go to shows or hunt or anything like that. It was great that I didn't have to jump today. You saved me, Bingle."

"Do you know Jill Crewe?" asked Lavender.

"No. But she met Porsche at some hunter trials last year. I've read all her books and she's a good rider. But, she lives in Scotland now."

"Occasionally she's down here in Oxfordshire. She goes back to Pool Cottage in Chatton to stay with her best friend, Ann Derry. Other times in the Highlands, where her step-father has Blainstock Castle!"

"That sounds rather grand. To tell the truth, I like the idea of a cute little cottage better," said Morgan.

"You said you didn't want to jump?" wondered Lavender. Then in a rush she went on, "my mother is obsessed with the idea of me winning competitions at gymkhanas. She's threatening to sell Bingle and buy me something more expensive. I'm desperate to hang on to him. I love him."

"Oh, poor you!" said Morgan sympathetically. "I don't get the thing about winning rosettes. We've got walls of them at home, not to mention cups lining mantelpieces in every room. Not won by me. By my golden brothers and sisters."

They got back to the horsebox, and Lavender found the picnic basket and offered Morgan an egg and cress sandwich. They tied up the ponies next to each other, so they could share a haynet.

"Lavender! You've raided the picnic lunch," said her mother huffing up behind them.

"Mummy," groaned Lavender. "I was hungry, and I can't eat in front of a visitor."

"Oh, Morgan! There you are. I've cancelled your entry. I was thinking perhaps Lavender and Black Boy might come over and stay with us for a few days. There's a week or so before the end of the holidays. That way, the ponies can spend some time together," said Aggie Pevensy rushing up, her hair escaping from its bun and framing her face in a wild tangle.

"Oh, no. I don't think that would be at all suitable," said Mrs E-H, drawing herself up straight.

"Oh, Mummy! Do say yes, think what fun it would be for them," cried Lavender.

"I'll tell you what, you consider it, and I'll come back later," said Aggie.

She walked away, smiling to herself. Mrs E-H thought the Pevensys too far beneath her. She was going to have to fix that. Her friend, Beryl Tainton was riding by, getting warmed up for the show hunter class.

"Beryl, dear. Can I ask a small favour of you?" she asked.

"Oh, Aggie. You know I would do anything for you," replied Beryl fondly.

They had a quick, whispered discussion, and Aggie pointed out where the Ellison-Heaths were parked.

Aggie walked on back to the large Pevensy horsebox. Both Mercedes and Porsche had horses here to compete in the open jumping and also the C-grade. She needed to help them get the horses ready as they had only brought one of the stable staff, Tom.

Mrs E-H was fuming. She didn't like the look of these people at all. They were trying to claim acquaintance. Of course, she was never going to let Lavender just go off and stay at the home of such badly dressed strangers.

"Where do you live?" she asked Morgan.

"We've got a place about five miles from Rychester."

"I see," said Mrs E-H, not having gleaned any useful information from this reply.

"Oh Morgan, sweetie," said Mrs Tainton riding up on a beautiful gleaming chestnut horse, kitted out in a double bridle with matching saddle. There were tiny little plaits along the crest of the horse's divinely curved neck.

"Oh hello, Mrs Tainton," said Lavender politely.

"Tell me, is your mother the Duchess of Tolkington here today? I wanted a word with her about the Parish Council. There's a meeting next week."

"She's probably over at the horse truck. It's parked over there, under those trees. She's helping Mercedes and Porsche get their horses ready." Morgan pointed to the other side of the parking area.

"Thank you, dear. I'll see you later," said Mrs Tainton riding away on her prancing, perfect horse.

Mrs E-H stood there as if struck by a large, jagged streak of enlightening lightning.

"Did she say your mother was the Duchess of Tolkington?" she asked Morgan. "Or is that some bizarre idea of a joke?"

"Yes, that was weird. Normally, she calls her Aggie. It was rather formal," said Morgan.

"Perhaps she wanted Mummy to know that she was a Duchess," said Lavender grinning. "But is she really a Duchess?"

"Yes, she is, and Daddy is a Duke. Why is that so important?" asked Morgan.

Lavender slid her eyes around and looked under her lashes at her mother.

"Mummy, why would that be important?"

She was taunting her mother. But Mrs E-H had suddenly seen a wonderful vista opening up before her eyes. A Duke and Duchess! Lavender's new best friend was the daughter of a Duke and Duchess! It was the most wonderful thing that had happened in years. She had to rush over and seal the deal.

She followed the direction that Morgan had pointed out and saw a huge horse truck with polished wood sides and gold and green paint spelling out "Pevensy Stables". She was racking her memory, Pevensy, Pevensy, she had never heard that name before, but she had certainly heard of the Duchess of Tolkington, who was often featured in the social pages of Tatler. She was the queen of good works in Oxfordshire. Such an acquaintance could open all the doors that to date had been shut firmly in her face.

"Good afternoon, Aggie," she said, stumbling over the woman's first name. She felt compelled to address her as Duchess and curtsey, but decided that as Aggie had introduced herself as Aggie, then that was the name she should use. "I'm sorry, I didn't introduce myself properly. I'm Evelyn Ellison-Heath, Lavender's mother."

"Evelyn, what a charming name," said Aggie, smiling warmly without a hint of cynicism. "Do sit down. Can I offer you a cup of tea or perhaps a glass of lemonade?"

"A cup of tea would be very welcome," said Evelyn obsequiously.

"Mummy, I'm going to take Tom over to the collecting ring with us. He can hold the horses while we walk the course.

Evelyn looked up at this vision of loveliness that must be one of Morgan's sisters.

"Who is that?" she asked Aggie.

"That's my daughter Mercedes, and then there's Porsche," said Aggie pointing out the other girl.

"She is divinely beautiful," laughed Evelyn in a sycophantic manner, admiring the girl's clear blue eyes and the most perfectly shaped pink mouth. Even with a riding cap, which has to be the most unbecoming of headgear, she was utter perfection.

"Yes, she is rather good-looking, certainly not last week's meatloaf. She does tend to put the rest of us in the shade."

Evelyn smiled. It suddenly occurred to her that there would be Pevensy sons, perhaps one that might marry Lavender. They could be childhood friends who fall in love. She imagined herself as the mother of the bride. Lavender would be a Duchess one day. She clasped her hands together rapturously at such a prospect of pure heaven.

"How many children do you have?" she asked, barely trying to hide her aspirations.

"I have five. The eldest boy is Royce, then Mercedes, Austin, Porsche and Morgan. All named after automobiles, which are my husband's passion."

"How original!" tooted Evelyn, positively pulsating with excitement. Perhaps Royce was too old, but Austin would be nearer Lavender's age. But Lavender would only be a Duchess if she married the elder son. But if there was another war, then Royce might be killed in action, and Austin would become the Duke.

"Have you considered whether Lavender and her pony might come and stay? I thought perhaps if they came on Tuesday. I've got the Vicar and his wife and some of the Parish council members coming for Sunday lunch tomorrow, and then I have to go to several rather tiresome committee meetings on Monday, but on Tuesday I'm free," said Aggie.

"Oh, that would be such fun. She would love it. She and Morgan seemed to have hit it off as much as the ponies," trilled Evelyn, not even conscious of the very obvious about-turn in her views.

"You must come for lunch when you drop her off!" said Aggie, turning on her heel to hide her amusement.

Suddenly, the stars were perfectly aligned. Evelyn floated back to give Lavender and Morgan the good news. Aggie watched Mrs E-H's departing back with a wry smile. She had her own agenda. A friend for Morgan who loved ponies and riding might just do the trick. To be rather plain and not a brilliant rider, the youngest of a large family of fantastic riders was an unkind cut of fortune. She hoped that Lavender might help Morgan get over her ridiculous dislike of equestrian competitions. Horses were the Pevensy family religion.

Chapter Six – Another Pony at Pool Cottage

On the way back to Chatton in the horsebox, there was no more discussion about selling Bingle. Mrs E-H now affected a huge devotion to the pony who had been the key to unlocking the door to her newfound friendship with the Duchess of Tolkington. And she had been told to call her Aggie. Dear Aggie!

Mr Ellison-Heath was somewhat bemused when he heard about the events at Chesterton. Listening to his wife's account of the reunion of Lavender's pony with his erstwhile best friend, Rapide, he was relieved. Perhaps now Evelyn might find her feet amongst the County set.

As Lavender went down for breakfast on Sunday morning, she was so excited at the prospect of staying at Morgan's house that she found herself twirling around like a ballerina, then pretending she was a horse she cantered and bucked, flinging her feet about like a lively colt. Bursting with excitement, she doubted that she would be able to sit through the Sunday morning service at St Michael's. Her mother had even suggested that they go to a church closer to Pevensy Park, perhaps the same one that dear Aggie attended.

"No, no, that would look far too obvious," said Lavender in an agony of embarrassment. If only her mother had not been invited to lunch on Tuesday. If she could just drop her and go.

After church, Lavender went up to her room and began to pack. She arranged her clothes neatly on the bed and chose the best of all her outfits. Selecting her edition of *Jill Has Two Ponies* from the shelf above her bed, she read again the account of how Rapide had been purchased from the wicked Joan Penberthy.

She had planned to give Bingle a day off after Chesterton Show, but he had hardly exerted himself with only two rounds and a half in the show jumping. She decided she would ride down to Mrs Darcy's and give Ruby a ride during her afternoon break.

The weather had turned gloomy, with scudding clouds and a distant hint of rain. It seemed that summer was over and autumn almost upon them. Bingle trotted up the road obediently. He didn't behave like a pony who had spontaneously exited the ring the day before.

"Oh! Bingle! You've found your best friend," said Lavender.

He tossed his head a little.

"You always understand what I'm saying to you," laughed Lavender. "And on Tuesday, we're going to stay at Pevensy Park, and you two can have a proper catch-up."

She was feeling happy. Her mother seemed to have entirely forgotten the evil plan to sell Bingle. Now he was the hero of the hour. The best thing since sliced bread! She was looking forward to going to the Pevensys. From what she gathered, it was horse heaven.

There was a lesson in progress when she arrived at Mrs Darcy's. Sunday afternoon was a popular time slot, and every pony was being ridden in a large circle around the schooling paddock. Lavender saw Ruby leading Mousie, with a very nervous-looking boy on board.

She sat on Bingle and watched from the gate. The riders were of mixed ability, and Serena was working hard to orchestrate a lesson that would suit all of them. She lined them up, and they did 'round the world', turning in their saddles. Then they had to lie back and rest the back of their heads on the ponies' rumps. Some of them were complaining that the edge of the cantle of the saddle was sticking into them. Then they were all sent to one side of the field, and they headed off in groups of five, trotting across to the other side. Ruby had to dash with Mousie's leading rein and managed to give instructions to the beginner rider, 'up, down, up, down,' helping him to get the rhythm to post to the trot.

The more advanced riders were then instructed to canter half a circle and pop over a small jump while the beginners watched. Serena called out instructions to each of them. The lesson finished with a walk, trot and canter relay race with the children shouting out encouragement to each other. Ponies who cantered when they should have been trotting had to turn a circle as a forfeit, and the riders were whirling them around frantically. They all clattered back to the yard, and Lavender could see Ruby darting from pony to pony, helping riders to put on their headcollars over the bridles and tying them to the rings that were embedded in the exterior stable walls. Girths were loosened, and Serena instructed some of the pupils to carry around water buckets so the ponies might drink. They would have an hour off before the final lesson of the day.

Parents were arriving to pick up their children, and Serena was in demand, answering questions. Wendy Mead was sitting at the desk inside the small office, took payments and scheduled the lessons for next week. When all the ponies were settled with water and girths loosened, Lavender went over to speak to Ruby.

"Would you like to ride Bingle for a bit until the next lesson," she asked.

"That, I would!" said Ruby, who seemed to be indefatigable, energy in abundance. She leapt on board, and Lavender helped her to adjust her stirrups.

Bingle trotted obediently around the ring. He had been ridden in this paddock for many years, not only with Jill but sometimes when he had been used for lessons with other riding school pupils. It was his old familiar territory.

While Ruby was trotting, Lavender shouted out her news at what had happened at Chesterton.

"I bin readin' them books about 'im, Black Boy that is, an' that Rapide," said Ruby. "They must have bin right glad to meet up agin."

"That they were," answered Lavender, adjusting her speech to mirror Ruby's.

The students for the next lesson were arriving, and Ruby had to resume her duties, tightening girths, adjusting stirrup lengths, reminding students of the correct procedure for mounting. Lavender stood back, so she didn't get in the way.

"Ruby, darling," said Serena, in her light, melodious voice. "There's no beginners who need leading in this lesson, so if you could stay back, the vet is arriving to check out Wendy's bay gelding in the far loose box. He's going to do his teeth and give him the once over."

Ruby saluted in mock military style. She and Lavender were to hang out in the yard awaiting the arrival of Henry Thurston. Lavender confided that now she had been invited to the Pevensys' place, her mother regarded Bingle as the hero of the hour.

The vet was late and skidded into the yard driving his disreputable old Land Rover. He had brought his girlfriend, Ann Derry, who was Jill Crewe's best friend. Lavender had never met her before, and she was very interested to see what she was like. Of course, she had read all about her in the Jill books, the way she had had a pony but hadn't like to ride much until Jill came along and enthused her. By all accounts, she was a merry, jolly girl.

Ruby carefully led out the big bay gelding, who was definitely the best-looking horse at the riding school.

"This is the 'orse you gotta look at," she said to Henry, her strange green eyes glittering with excitement at the responsibility she'd been given. Then Wendy rushed into the yard.

"Oh Wendy, so good to see you. What's up?" said Ann. "Henry says that he's to give your bay horse a check-up. What's his name?"

"Bright Eyes," said Wendy.

"He's a beauty," said Ann.

"What are you riding yourself?" asked Wendy.

"I've got that ex-steeplechaser, Black Comedy. You know the one that Jill rode in the point-to-point. He's a dear old fellow. Now that Jill has taken Balius and Skydiver back to Scotland, he's all alone in the field. He wanders around disconsolately."

"Did you hear that Bingle, well really Black Boy, he and Rapide met up with each other yesterday at Chesterton Show," burst out Lavender.

"Do tell!" exclaimed Ann.

"I was riding Bingle, well Black Boy, in a jumping event, and suddenly he neighed very loudly and dashed out through the exit and into the collecting ring. He'd found Rapide."

"Oh! What a clever boy he is!" exclaimed Ann, clasping her hands together. "Those two were always the best of friends. I know that originally Jill sold them to the same family so that they could stay together, but something went wrong, and they were sold on to separate owners."

"I'm going to stay with Rapide's new family for a few days so that they can spend some time together."

"I thought that Rapide was owned by Porsche Pevensy," said Ann.

"Yes, that's right. But now he's being ridden by the youngest girl, Morgan. She's about my age."

"The Pevensys are a wonderful family, I've heard," said Ann. "Henry, you know Royce, don't you?"

"Yes, we were at the local school together when we were young 'uns, but then he went off to some fancy boarding school. I have to say, he's a good chap. Writes poetry, you know," said Henry, as he was running his finger up and down the edge of Bright Eyes' teeth to see if there were any sharp edges that needed filing.

"You know there's old Tottie in the back paddock. He's been retired now. He'd be an ideal companion horse. Why don't you take him back to Pool Cottage to hang out with your big horse?" said Wendy thoughtfully.

"What a brilliant idea!" said Ann, brightly. "I remember him, he was one of the best, especially at bending. How old would he be now?"

"He's well over twenty but still quite a spritely gentleman," said Wendy. "He was one of Mrs Darcy's favourites. Ruby would you mind running down the back paddock and catching him up."

Ruby and Lavender went into the tack room, found a halter and walked down to the paddock where the cross-country jumps were scattered across the side of the hill.

"He looks really old," said Ruby, "kind of moth-eaten."

"Imagine all the children that he has taught to ride," said Lavender, who felt that it was important to venerate the older generations.

"He's absolutely perfect," trilled Ann when they got back to the stable yard. Tottie stepped out with dignity. He obviously didn't consider himself a total has-been. Perhaps he thought that he was to be pressed back into service for the last Sunday lesson of the day.

"Will Lavender and I lead 'im down to ya place?" suggested Ruby boldly.

"Would you, that would be so kind. It's not far, you know, and it would be a lot easier than using a horse trailer. Do you know where Pool Cottage is?"

"Surely we do," said Ruby.

Lavender was excited. She had long wanted to have a look around Pool Cottage, where so many of Jill Crewe's childhood adventures had been staged.

"Oughta, we go now?" asked Ruby.

"Yes, do," said Wendy. "Serena and I can manage to finish up here. If you go now before all the children and their parents descend on us."

Lavender fetched Bingle, and they set off.

"I'll lead him if you like. You can ride Bingle," she said to Ruby kindly.

They arrived at Pool Cottage at the same time as Ann and Henry. The twilight was stretching across the fields like long fingers. The trees were beginning to lose their leaves which twirled through the evening breeze. The horizon was smudged a misty-blue.

"Bring him around to the stable and let's introduce him to Black Comedy," said Ann.

They walked down the driveway and round the back. There were two loose boxes, just as had been described in the Jill books. An orchard and a small field.

"This is so perfect," sighed Lavender, wishing that her own house had this homely feeling.

"Yes, it is cosy, very picture-book," said Ann.

"You are lucky to live here," said Lavender wistfully, thinking of her uncomfortable, modernised house that always seemed so soulless.

Black Comedy snuffed the air with delight at the arrival of two other equine beings. He rumbled deep in his throat and stretched his nose down to sniff at the diminutive pony that was led up to him to be introduced. Tottie stood there in a dignified manner. Henry ran his hand down the little pony's back. His backbone was beginning to protrude a little, and his ribs were showing.

"Was they not feedin' 'im prop'ly?" asked Ruby, who was not backwards in coming forwards.

"No, not at all, he's just old, his body shape is showing it," replied Henry, certainly not wanting to be caught out criticising the people at Mrs Darcy's. "I'll have a word with one of my colleagues, and we'll come up with a diet that should help him. I'll just run the rasp over his teeth now, and take off a few of the edges. His hoofs are looking good. Perhaps you two young ones could get yourself a rasp and have a go at keeping them in good order."

"Can normal people file hoofs?" asked Lavender in astonishment. She had always thought that was up to the blacksmith.

"I don't see why not. It might be a useful skill in the future for young horsewomen such as yourselves," said Henry, whose father had been something of a jack of all trades.

Lavender was quick to pick up that Henry and Ann were including them in the future plans for old Tottie. She was secretly thrilled to be pulled into a bunch of people, to be one of the group was something that seemed to have eluded her all her life. She blamed her mother with her strident and unattractive manners, but secretly she had always wondered if there was something in her that was not like other people.

"I'll buy a file next time I'm in town and then all three of us can have a go, under your masterful direction of course, Henry," said Ann, smiling at him mischievously.

"You'd best be riding home Lavender, it's getting dark. Henry can run Ruby back to her place on his way home," said Ann.

Lavender leapt back onto Bingle and trotted down the country lanes. Her mother would be peevish that she had been away so long. She would tell her about what had happened, but she knew that the significance of this new responsibility for such a noble old pony as Tottie would entirely pass her mother by.

Chapter Seven – Dressing Up

When Lavender arrived home, Mrs E-H was on the phone with her god-daughter, Susan King, telling her the news about the forthcoming lunch at Pevensy Park.

"Oh darling!" gushed Susan. "You absolutely must have something new to wear, and you can be my first customer!"

"Your first customer?" asked Mrs E-H, for a moment diverted from her stream of thought.

"Yes, I start my new job tomorrow morning. It's a darling boutique right in the middle of Oxford. If it all works out, then I plan to open my own shop!"

"Oh! Goodness!" exclaimed Mrs E-H. Her mind was racing. She wasn't sure that a woman working was quite the thing, but an upmarket boutique in Oxford, might be considered acceptable. She had heard quite a lot about women having careers and their own businesses lately.

"Do come and visit! I start at nine in the morning but give me an hour or so to learn the ropes. Think how impressed dear Cynthia will be if I sell my first outfit before lunch. And the clothes there are to die for! We'll find you a darling little frock, or perhaps a natty suit that will give you just the right look for lunch at Pevensy Park!"

Susan hung up the mustard-coloured Bakelite phone, carefully untwirling the spiral cable that seemed to get twisted up every time she used it. She wasn't sure how she felt about her godmother's sudden ascent up the social scale. If Lavender became best friends with Morgan Pevensy, that would be a previously unimaginable shift in the social universe. Surely, it had to be a good thing for herself. She might also be admitted into the Pevensy circle. Perhaps she might take up horse riding again. It could be the perfect entrée.

Susan was still raw from her utter humiliation at Chatton Show. It was ironic that Barty, who was so rarely demonstrative, had come out of his shell and assaulted her while she was commentating in the most embarrassing manner possible. During the last week, she had found herself involuntarily shuddering at the memory, swamped with mortification and shame. She had cut herself off from her usual social circle. They were her dear friends, but they would have heartlessly enjoyed teasing her about the incident.

The opportunity to work three days a week in Cynthia's boutique, called Creations, had been a welcome diversion. It might be just the thing. She felt the desire to move beyond Rychester, into a wider world. Jill Crewe's dressage display had touched a nerve, even before the debacle during the actual event. It was a worrisome toothache that had now reached epic proportions. Jill had always been sidey, and now this latest stunt of hers was in utterly bad taste. Who did she think she was – a dressage expert!

Susan supposed it was that stupendous horse. Jill had spent her childhood messing around on, quite frankly, second-rate ponies. Her old adversary's surprise move to a castle in the Highlands of Scotland with a rich stepfather who was some sort of chieftain had certainly been an unwelcome leap, but as it was so far away from Oxfordshire, it barely counted. Money might have helped improve Jill's quality of horses, but perversely this had confirmed Susan's long-held belief that the price one paid for a horse was a sure indicator of its worth and quality.

Dressage! Pah! Her father, George Pyke, was one of the old school. He thought that dressage was new-fangled rubbish and ought to be banished back to the Continent where it had come from, infecting decent, upstanding hunting folk in Britain. The English were the best horsemen in the world. Everyone knew that!

Susan had deliberated for hours on what she should wear on her first day of work and had finally decided on a smart navy-blue suit that her mother had bought for her before the wedding. It was stylish but understated. She assumed that Cynthia would be kitting her out in 'Creations' stock if it all worked out. It made sense that she should be displaying the wares to their customers.

On Monday morning at breakfast, she passed Barty the toast expecting him to comment on her outfit and her first day at work, but he had hidden himself behind *The Times*. She suppressed a faint whisper of disappointment. It was almost as if Barty had dismissed her as a silly woman, playing at a ridiculous career.

"Barty, darling, do you know any of the Pevensys?" she asked as she carefully buttered a piece of toast and spooned marmalade onto the side of the plate.

"The eldest son, Royce, was up at Oxford with one of the junior partners. He is something of a wastrel, always dashing about the countryside, and then off sailing in the summer. He writes poetry," replied Barty in a voice tinged with sneering disapproval.

Susan looked at her husband carefully. Royce sounded like the perfect friend for them. Who cared if he didn't have a serious profession, he would inherit the title and be a Duke! Sometimes, she wondered if Barty wasn't just a touch too middle class in his notions. She would have to help him lift his sights a little and aspire to a more glamorous social life.

She suppressed the worrisome thought that she might have aimed higher in choosing a husband. At the time, she had thought that Barty was rather a catch, but perhaps she had been wrong. One of her friends, Priscilla, had been angling for his attention, and in a fit of capricious spite, Susan had set her cap at him. Barty hadn't bothered with Priscilla again and turned all his attention to Susan, who felt as if she were winning a competition. Before she knew it, they were engaged, and she was swept down the aisle without much serious consideration. Sometimes, in the still watches of the night when she woke and couldn't go back to sleep, it occurred to her that perhaps she had been too hasty. Might she have done better?

In the clear light of day, she focused on the idea of climbing the social ladder, consorting with the upper classes. She had a surprisingly detailed vision of Barty and herself cruising with a select group of friends around the Greek islands. In her idle moments, she embroidered this imagined scenario. They would be rowed ashore and lunch in a charming fishing village built on the steep slopes above a harbour. In her daydream, she could feel the molten summer heat and the soft, languorous air. The table would be set with local food in the deep shade of an overhanging building, a pergola of vine giving dappled shade in the garden beside them. In the distance, the purple sea glittered in the sun blazing down from a sapphire sky. The sea birds would dive or hang on flashing wings, and the wavelets would make a silvery shirring sound on the sand. They would enjoy the view of picturesque, local fishermen sleeping in the shade of their upturned boats amongst a tangle of nets of tackle beside a slipway.

In her imagination, they would loll in sybaritic pleasure, their minds attuned to the perfect summer haze of being abroad. Barty would make witty, amusing remarks and the others would laugh at his cleverness. All would be right in their small select world.

It may seem strange to readers of the early Jill books that Susan Pyke (now King) should have such a romantic dreamy bent. Jill had represented her as a sharp, materialistic, sarcastic girl who always referred to the worst possible view of those around her. Perhaps she had always had this mentality but had hidden it behind a steely exterior? Alternatively, it was a new progression since the disappointments of her marriage.

No matter where this dream had come from, Susan was certain that she could accomplish it. She wasn't sure that working in a boutique in Oxford was a step in the right direction, but anything was better than mouldering in their neat new house. She had to get out there and make things happen. Working in an upmarket frock shop would mean meeting new people. It was an intriguing turn of events, Lavender and Evelyn falling in with the Pevensys, perhaps a conjunction that boded well for the future. Of course, she had known of the celebrated and titled Pevensys for many years, but they were that little too far from Chatton to be considered local, and their charmed lives had shimmered on the distant horizon. Now they were tantalisingly within reach. She hoped that Evelyn would include her in some social event so that she might meet them officially, and from there, who knew where it might lead?

Barty dropped her off at the station on his way to work, and she caught the train to Oxford. The boutique was only a ten-minute brisk walk from the station. She adored Oxford. The colleges, the Bridge of Sighs, the secret, winding tiny lanes that emerged suddenly into cobbled streets, the very old buildings and of course, the dreaming towers and spires. Her heels clip-clopped on the pavement in a most satisfying manner, and she felt as if she were marching to meet her fate. The first step on the rung of the ladder to success.

When she arrived at the shop, Cynthia was pleased to see her. She was a middle-aged matron who had been denied the joy of children and had concentrated on her business. Her husband was a local doctor. They enjoyed an active social life in Oxford with other professionals, but not the staff at the colleges. They were quite a different set, the intellectuals. Cynthia was outfitted in one of the tweedy autumn outfits that were part of her newest collection.

"I do love winter clothes," she tweeted, running her hands down the finely woven fabrics, "there's something so satisfying about wool and cashmere. And a new winter coat always gives one such a boost. I imagine you'll be spending your whole wage on outfits. I'll give you a generous staff discount, of course."

Susan smiled at her warmly. Obviously, free outfits were not going to be part of the deal. Nevertheless, she did like Cynthia. She was a very smart woman. Not overweight or fusty, she had not let herself go. Her figure was trim, her hair carefully coiffed, light makeup subtly applied and discreet jewellery, a string of pearls, jewelled rings on her fingers and carefully manicured nails.

After Susan had been shown the small back office, the kitchenette where they made tea for the favoured customers, the plush little banquette where the odd husband was parked if he had been dragged along by his wife, and the mysterious workings of the enormous cash register, Cynthia suggested that she look through the racks of clothes to familiarise herself with the stock.

"The trick is to assess the woman's shape and steer her towards something flattering. You would be amazed at how some women just cannot choose the right outfit for themselves. Tact is the name of the game!"

"I can see how that would work," said Susan.

"You know that most of your salary will be commission-based, so the more sales you make, the more money in your pay packet," said Cynthia briskly.

Susan continued to smile brightly, but inside, her heart was sinking. She realised that she would be working as nothing more than a glorified shopgirl. She couldn't remember why she had thought this a good idea. She imagined Jill Crewe and Ann Derry breezing in and finding her working there. They would have a terrific time trying on outfits and making fun of her. She would have to be polite and servile. It would be utterly humiliating. Her stomach was fluttering with nerves. Her judgement since she had left school seemed to have taken her along a life course that was utterly at odds with what she had imagined for herself. She should be the one that was invited to lunch at Pevensy Park, laughing and gossiping with the Duchess of Tolkington and riding out with Mercedes and Austin.

As if on cue, Evelyn rushed into the shop, with little Lavender trailing behind her.

"Oh, Susan! How terribly fortuitous that you should be working here. You absolutely must find me the perfect outfit for lunch at Pevensy Park," said her godmother with her ghastly accent and strangled vowels.

It was all Susan could do to smile politely with at least an attempt at warmth.

"Something for lunch at Pevensy Park," she repeated, looking over at Cynthia. This would be her sale, but she hoped she might receive some direction from her new boss.

"Oh, dear Aggie!" Cynthia cried. Apparently, everyone in Oxford was friends with the Duchess except herself, thought Susan wryly. This was too much. She was squirming inside and only just managing to maintain a cool demeanour.

The outfit that Cynthia presented to Evelyn as 'just the thing', was supposedly the height of fashion for this autumn. It was a gold corduroy knickerbocker suit worn with school-grey knee socks and a high polo-collared jersey. Topped with a knitted grey hat, a bitter-chocolate midcalf coat with split sides and a leather belt, with the finishing touch of a knitted grey scarf. It wasn't something that Susan would have dared to wear, and she was a good twenty-five years younger than her godmother. Susan thought Evelyn was going to look utterly ridiculous but managed to keep a smile on her face and nod encouragingly for at least five minutes. Then, she turned to Lavender to distract herself from this gruesome piece of play-acting.

"Your mother has told me that the youngest girl owns Rapide now," she said.

"Yes, he and Bingle were so sweet, they were just made to be together," said Lavender.

"I remember when Jill owned both of them," said Susan evenly. She was careful not to be catty about Jill as Lavender was a fan. "You know Jill and I were point and counter-point when we were competing in the gymkhanas."

Lavender had no idea what she was talking about. She was pretty sure that Jill might have looked similarly bemused. Susan seemed to be trying to dress-up her relationship with Jill as something sophisticated, not just two high-spirited school girls who had not hit it off.

"Mummy has promised me a new riding outfit, so I can look smart when I'm staying at Morgan's place," said Lavender confidingly.

"I'm not sure that you're meant to dress up like a horse show when you're staying with a friend," said Susan. "But you might want something special to wear for dinner. Or will you be eating in the nursery with nanny?"

"I have no idea," said Lavender. "But I'll make sure to pack some good clothes. I'll let Mummy buy me the riding clothes, but I don't suppose I'll wear them. I'll keep them for the next show."

"Smart girl," said Susan approvingly.

Mrs E-H left with her new outfit, a huge smile on her face. She was thrilled.

"Do I get commission on those sales?" asked Susan.

"Darling, I'm not sure that I appreciate that attitude. I did choose them for her. Let's go half and half in the commission," said Cynthia.

The afternoon dragged. Several customers came in, but Cynthia helped them choose their clothes and Susan was instructed to make cups of tea. She absolutely hated it. This was just not for her. She decided that she'd make an excuse and not come back. There was no way she was going to spend her days making cups of tea for annoying middle-aged women who treated her like a servant. What had she been thinking?

On the way back to the station, she lingered in the High Street. She was in no hurry to get home. In the bookshop window was a display of Jill Crewe's books. Taking a deep breath, she plunged into the shop and bought all five of the adult stories, *Jill Rides Cross-Country, Jill Has Two Horses, Jill Goes Pony Trekking, Jill and the Steeplechaser,* and *Jill Dreams of a Dressage Horse.* She was saved the ignominy of knowing that she had been spotted by Ann Derry, who was ferreting around at the back of the shop, looking for an obscure volume about veterinary science that Henry had mentioned. She saw Susan purchase Jill's books and had to cover her mouth to stop herself hooting with laughter. Wait until she told Jill. She would be beyond gobsmacked!

Susan arrived home before Barty was back from the office and defiantly changed into a pair of comfortable slacks and an old sweater. She didn't care if Barty liked to see her dressed up and lipsticked upon his return from the office. Hang Barty with his half-boiled expectations! She had prepared the vegetables and put some chops under the grill. The table was set, and she turned on the television so Barty could watch the news when he came in.

Over dinner, Barty seemed to have entirely forgotten that she had spent a day working in Oxford. Either he just didn't care, or he thought it was beneath his notice. Susan didn't bring up the subject. She didn't want to admit that she had hated it and wasn't going back. She planned to ring Cynthia in the morning and explain that she just wasn't up to it.

"You did remember that we have invited Mr Alcott to dinner next week with his wife," said Barty as he carefully cut up his vegetables.

"Yes, darling," she replied meekly. "I am working on a menu."

He smiled at her approvingly.

"I've decided that working at Creations is really just not me. I'm going to ring Cynthia tomorrow and tell her," she said.

"Absolutely right. You're hardly cut out to be a shop assistant," he said smugly.

This infuriated her to the point where she might almost have gone back on her decision and continued working, but that would have been self-defeating. She needed to think again. She had to find herself a role. Barty went straight to sleep that night. The romance component of their marriage seemed to have been reduced to nil. Tentatively she picked up Jill's first adult book, *Jill Rides Cross-Country*. She opened it warily as if it were an unexploded bomb. She knew that she would feature in the story and she hated to think of how Jill might have portrayed her. But she couldn't help thinking that perhaps Jill really did have the answers to a fun life, but it was hard to admit this. Mentally she held her nose as she dived into the first chapter.

Chapter Eight – Lunch with the Duke and Duchess

Mrs E-H was now kitted out in her new outfit, and Lavender found it hard to keep a straight face. Quite frankly, her mother looked ridiculous. If she had been a gorgeous young twenty-year-old socialite from London, she might have carried it off, but there was no denying that she was nothing but a small-town middle-aged matron. Lavender wished with all her heart that her mother had not been invited to lunch. If only she could just drop her off with Bingle and her suitcase and tack and go. Her mother acting posh was like a flapping goldfish that had leapt out of its bowl.

They followed the directions that Aggie had given them, driving down the main street of Rychester and then winding around a road that led to a tiny village called Langton Shrove. This was a picturesque community. On the outskirts were some tumbledown houses and farm sheds that gave it a touch of the archaic. Small cottages that were probably part of the Pevensy estate, sheltered behind hedges and under the boughs of huge oak trees. Through the village, a mile further on were the gates to Pevensy Park. They were suitably grand, with tall gateposts topped with gryphons. There was a small lodge house with bright blue and egg yolk-yellow curtains, with a door painted pillar box-red.

"What a sweet little cottage!" exclaimed Lavender. "Just like a doll's house."

"Look at this park!" enthused her mother, taking in the huge expanse of green velvet grass with large oak trees, their leaves beginning to turn russet.

The road curved to the left and then to the right. There were cross-country jumps dotted here and there.

"This is horse paradise," breathed Lavender.

They glimpsed a tall bay gelding with a rider cantering between the distant trees. Then the horsebox rounded the last curve, and there was the house laid out before them.

"Oh, what a charming establishment!" exclaimed Evelyn. It was even more impressive than she had imagined. The house was huge, with half a dozen sections of buildings stretched before them in delicious golden sandstone with handsome chimneys reaching into the sky, glittering windows, and carved wooden doors.

Morgan danced down the front steps towards them, leaping about like an elf on her very thin legs.

"Follow the road around to the stables. I'll show you," she called, running in front of them.

In Lavender's eyes, the stables were even more impressive than the house. They were palatial. The yard was arranged with loose boxes on three sides. The large Pevensy horsebox was parked off to the side. There were yards under a cluster of trees and small fenced fields beyond that.

"Park here! Park here!" shouted Morgan leaping about like a dervish and pointing to a place beside the big Pevensy horsebox.

In a trice, Bingle was unloaded, and Tom, the groom who had been at Chesterton Show, led him to a loose box beside Rapide, who was whinnying at the top of his voice. The two ponies could just touch noses over the top of the half-doors, and they whiffled and snorted in their own horse language.

"They love each other so much," said Morgan. "I wonder what they're actually saying to each other. If only we could understand horse talk. I thought we might turn them out in a field together after lunch."

"That's a good idea," said Lavender, wondering if she might suggest that they ride around that fabulous park first.

"Come in for lunch. Mummy instructed Cook to prepare something sumptuous," said Morgan.

Mrs E-H was quivering with expectation and nervousness, clutching her smart crocodile-skin handbag in a tense grip. There were knots in her stomach. She was very conscious that she had never before eaten a meal with any member of the aristocracy. She believed that her whole future was going to be determined by the way that she wielded her knife and fork at lunch.

Morgan led them back from the stables to the house. They took a path through a tunnel of gleaming green leafy shrubbery and entered a side door that took them into a corridor that opened up into a high cavernous hall that led into another long corridor.

"This is like a stately home," said Lavender in tones of wonder.

"Shhh," hissed her mother, not wanting to be shown up.

Aggie had the measure of Evelyn and had arranged for lunch to be served in a rather grand, small formal dining room. The walls were wood, polished the colour of hot cocoa, sectioned into octagonal panels. The ceiling plaster was vaulted and embellished by swirls and medallions. A dozen paintings hung close to each other along the walls, each bordered with an intricate wooden, gilt-edged frame. All pastoral scenes lit up with individual lights as if they were in an art gallery. A Chippendale mahogany dining table was trimmed with vanilla satinwood.

Aggie had insisted that her husband attend and had also rounded up the children who were home. Mercedes had gone down to London for several days, and Royce was up in Scotland blasting away at birds somewhere on the moor. But Austin and Porsche were home and were told that they should be there on time. She had instructed the cook to serve three courses and use the third-best china and cutlery. She even made an effort to achieve the appearance of a Duchess at home with a soft cashmere pullover and well-cut wool skirt with a priceless, glowing, lustrous string of black pearls around her neck.

She met her guests coming down the corridor and hurried forward.

"I expected Morgan to bring you in the front door, but do come in. Lunch is about to be served."

The Duke of Tolkington was hovering in the doorway of the dining room. He was a gentle-mannered man who lived in his own dream world of automobiles. He was not much interested in people, the total opposite of his wife who loved all sorts of humans and found them endlessly fascinating. He left all the people things to Aggie, who was always planning and scheming, in the nicest possible way. If it didn't turn out the way she had wanted then she could change course in a flash and go with another idea. She was keen to impress this woman who was dressed up in these most extraordinary clothes. It was all about a special friend for Morgan. Aggie was still determined that she could turn their youngest into a horsewoman of the same ilk as her brothers and sisters. Personally, the Duke had rather liked the fact that Morgan was interested in cars and shared his bent towards mechanics, but he dared not thwart his wife in her desires.

"Do sit down, Evelyn," said Aggie, in her best hostess voice, warm and inviting. "Perhaps next to Louis, my husband."

Austin and Porsche entered together. The two of them created quite a presence. Half of the quartet of the golden brothers and sisters that Morgan had wryly described. Self-assurance emanated from them like a tidal wave. Lavender stared in fascination.

"Porsche, Austin, this is Evelyn and Lavender Ellison-Heath, my second eldest son and my second eldest daughter."

Porsche and Austin joined the group at the table, good-looking and laughing with the easy confidence of those born with half a dozen silver spoons in their well-bred mouths. Porsche was a heavenly apparition with softly glowing strawberry-blond hair that artfully framed her flawless face. Austin was perhaps not conventionally handsome, but his boyish face was creased in merriment, and he exuded goodwill to all mankind. A half-smile played hide-and-seek around the corners of his wide mouth, and his eyes crinkled attractively at the corners. Looking at these young members of the aristocracy, it was possible to believe that they were the product of a mixture of the bloodlines of the gods and humans, born to be privileged, to rule and be blessed in every worldly way. Certainly, Evelyn believed in the myth of aristocracy.

"Which is Evelyn, and which is Lavender?" asked Austin in a jaunty tone that nearly crossed the line into rudeness, but somehow his charming smile smoothed over any possible offence.

"I'm Evelyn," said Mrs E-H, smiling in a gruesomely flirtatious manner, "and this is my daughter Lavender."

"How do you do?" asked Porsche.

"Please, everyone, do sit down. You know how peeved Cook is if we're not seated ready for lunch to be served. Mrs Milner, our Cook is an absolute wonder, but she has a thing about punctuality," said Aggie.

Privately, Mrs E-H thought that Aggie needed to get a hold of the servants. They were to serve the family, not to lay down strictures on time-keeping!

"Lavender, it's good to meet you. Your pony is quite famous, you know, through Jill Crewe's books," said Porsche. Aggie stared at her daughter, who was being uncharacteristically congenial today.

"I know," replied Lavender. "Morgan said that you met Jill at some hunter trials. Jill gave me some riding lessons a while ago."

"I see that Jill has been writing for *Horse and Hound*," said Austin. "I loved her piece about the Clutterbucks."

"The name Clutterbuck is rather charming," murmured Aggie. "I remember going to school with an Eleanor Clutterbuck."

Evelyn sat there listening with her mouth agape. She was conscious that she did not have that effortless grace and sense of entitlement that rippled around the table. She would never admit it, hardly allowed the thoughts to enter her head, but she was from humble beginnings. Lavender had never even met her grandparents, who lived in a dingy terrace house in Stoke-on-Trent. They ate a lot of oatcakes. Evelyn's stomach turned at the mere thought of a stodgy oatcake dripping with bacon fat. She had always known that she was born for a different life. Marrying Mr Ellison-Heath, (a double-barrelled name!) had been a huge step up, but somehow she hadn't really achieved her goal until now.

Everyone sat, and Mrs E-H found herself seated very agreeably between the charming and handsome young Austin and Louis, no less than a Duke! She was tittering with delight. Aggie smiled benevolently. She felt sure that this was all going to work out very well.

Mrs E-H had read somewhere that topics of conversation in country houses should be about 'weather, dogs and gardens' and perhaps in this household, one could include horses. She tried valiantly to talk about the weather, but only the most inane comments came to mind, and she was too overcome to speak them.

Lunch was delicious. The first course was fish mousse drizzled with lemon sauce, served with tiny triangles of toast. Lavender had no idea what type of fish it was, perhaps a mixture, but it tasted like nothing she had ever eaten before. The next course was as meaty and hearty as the first had been light and airy. Medallions of beef, cooked to perfection, browned on the outside and pink on the inside, with a delicious mushroom sauce, small roasted potatoes and steamed vegetables, served individually to each person by a very tactful member of staff expertly wielding a silver fork and spoon.

Lavender wondered fleetingly whether the Pevensys ate like this every lunchtime or whether it was a special menu served for visitors. She had imagined it would all be good stolid John Bull food but this was like something that might be served in an upmarket London restaurant.

"Do you think we could ride after lunch?" asked Lavender, as they were scraping their dessert bowls for the last of the divine summer pudding served with thick clotted cream.

"I suppose so," said Morgan, who knew that she had to be polite and cater for her guest's desires. Aggie smiled. Her plan was working.

Chapter Nine – Riding Rapide

The girls scampered down to the stables and brought out the tack.

"Why don't we swap ponies?" suggested Morgan. "You can try Rapide if you like, and I wouldn't mind riding lovely Black Boy, I mean Bingle, I feel as if I know him after reading Jill's books."

"Yes, if you like," replied Lavender eagerly. She was keen to try out Rapide's jumping abilities, to see how much he had changed his original cat-jumping technique, which had been a product of the evil Joan Penberthy's torturous training techniques.

They mounted.

"Would you like to ride around the park?" asked Morgan, "or we could go up to the woods?"

Lavender got the feeling that Morgan preferred the park to a longer hack through the woods.

"The park would be good," she said, "perhaps we could try some of the cross-country jumps that I saw when we drove in."

They set off. Lavender had not ridden many horses, as Bingle was her first pony, and she had more or less learnt on him. Rapide's stride was longer than Bingle's, and she felt further from the ground. He was also a little more lively. She could sense his eagerness and *joie-de-vivre*. But all the same, he was so well-schooled that she didn't feel as if he were going to run away with her.

"Do you think I should change Bingle's name back to Black Boy?" she asked while they walked from the stables along the track that circumnavigated the park, which was at least five acres.

"Yes, I do," said Morgan. "Like changing the name of a boat, it might be bad luck."

"Then that is what I'll do. Perhaps it will help us win more rosettes to keep Mummy happy," she said dolefully.

"*My* mother wants me to compete all the time. It's not so much the rosettes, something about the family honour," said Morgan. "To tell you the truth, I wouldn't mind if I never had to ride in a gymkhana or show ever again. I'm just not the same as the others. Mercedes is the best rider. I think she wants to get to the Olympics, although she doesn't boast about it, but I'm sure it is her ambition. And Porsche is desperately competitive, determined to beat

Mercedes, who everybody loves. Austin bothers with nothing but point-to-point races, the thrill of the speed and the thunder of hoofs and all that."

"Is there something else that you like doing?" asked Lavender.

"Well, I love the cars, and secretly, Daddy lets me drive now and again, and I help him with the mechanical things. I'm learning how an engine works," said Morgan proudly. "Then there's my drawing. I have a whole collection that I've done, mainly animals. That's my thing."

Lavender smiled a little at this. It was in line with a lot of the pony books she'd read. Often the heroine of the story was artistic. She remembered in one story by Joanna Cannan, the mother of the famous Pullein Thompson sisters, the girl had earned money through selling her pictures. Perhaps Morgan was inadvertently following the storylines of the pony book life.

"Do you want to jump Rapide?" asked Morgan as a wide brush jump came into view. It was placed beside the track, and if you wanted to jump, you followed a branching path to the left. At one end, it was only two feet six, then a leap to about three feet six and then at the other end, a huge four feet.

"These jumps are fantastic," breathed Lavender in ecstasy. "I suppose your brothers and sisters use them for training their horses."

"Yes, mostly Mercedes, she's very keen on three-day eventing, has been for years. She has this funny dressage coach called Pierre St Marchand. He used to be in the Cadre Noir in France, which is a special place for horse training, I believe."

"That must be amazing. You know Jill is getting into dressage now, with that new horse of hers, Skydiver. She did this exhibition thing at Chatton Show. She came round to our place once with him, and showed me how he went."

"Yes, I heard something about that. The lady commentating got involved in some rather noisy romantic activity, and everyone around the showground heard it," said Morgan.

"I'm afraid that was my Aunt Susan. She's Mummy's god-daughter," replied Lavender.

"That's not Susan Pyke from the Jill books, is it? Gosh, that's funny," said Morgan, chuckling.

"I'm going to try and jump, just the low end," said Lavender, suddenly ashamed of her family's affiliation with the dreaded Susan Pyke. "Is there anything I should know before I have a go?"

"No, just tell him to go forward and over he goes. He's pretty good at it. I'll ride around, so he's coming up behind us, now that these two have decided that they're inseparable."

Lavender shortened her stirrup leathers by a couple of holes, gathered up her reins and trotted a circle. She felt unaccountably nervous about this but terribly excited at the same time.

Rapide flicked his ears back and forward as if to say 'don't worry' and set off at a fast canter. He was much livelier than her faithful Bingle, or Black Boy as she had now decided to call him. She sat quite still, fighting the temptation to try and slow him down, and they soared over the brush jump at the low end, some twelve inches higher than they needed to clear it. She grabbed at the mane and stayed on. Morgan was laughing at her.

"He loves jumping, it's his favourite thing!"

"Yes, he is very keen," said Lavender, laughing now she had done it. Heady exhilaration was flowing through her body.

"Take him back around and go over the middle section. You would have jumped that high anyway," said Morgan.

Lavender took a deep breath, deciding that if she were ever to be a good horsewoman, she needed to buck up and ride courageously. Taking a fresh hold on the reins, keeping a firm contact, she remembered something she had read about how much you had to feel the horse's mouth. It was like holding hands. If you're walking, then your grip on each other is relatively loose, but if you start to run, then you tighten your grasp. Rapide was getting into his stride now, and he beetled confidently towards the jump, up and over, a leap that cleared the brush easily but wasn't extravagant.

"Come on," called Morgan, "we can canter on, and you can go over all the jumps. There is at least a dozen of them. All different designs."

"I feel like I'm riding at Badminton," called Lavender, breathless with excitement.

Black Boy cantered ahead, and Lavender noticed how well Morgan sat a horse. She did seem like a natural rider. It was so strange that she didn't really care for riding much. They rode on, over three sets of post-and-rails, then a hedge that had been cut at different heights, then large tree trunks, followed by a series of water jumps at the stream. You had to jump over one of the fences that lined the bank, into the water, four strides across the gravelly bottom and then leap up a bank, and one stride onto another fence, or you could swing to the left and go over a bounce, two jumps so close together that there were no strides between them. Rapide leapt down into the water, and Lavender only just stayed on board. No wonder there were so many falls at water jumps where the crowds always gathered, hoping to view some splashy action.

There was a stone wall after that and then some barrels lying on their sides, and even a little set of wooden structures that were painted with chimneys

to look like a row of huts. Obviously, Rapide had jumped them all before when Porsche had been riding him, but he was still eager and leapt everything in front of him with great enthusiasm.

"Gosh! He is utterly fantastic!" gasped Lavender. "It's like he inspires me totally. I just want to jump higher and higher."

"You're as bad as the rest of them," said Morgan in a mocking voice, but she was smiling. It was fine for the others, it just wasn't her.

They got back to the stables and Tom came out to take the ponies.

"It's alright, we'll look to them," said Morgan.

They untacked and set to rubbing them down.

"They're starting to get their winter coats," said Lavender.

"Yes, thank goodness, it's the end of the show season. I'll be back to school soon," commented Morgan.

"What's it like at boarding school?" asked Lavender. "I mean, I've read a lot of school stories, Enid Blyton, Angela Brazil and all that, and it does sound rather jolly with midnight feasts and mysteries."

"It's not quite the same as in books, but it's alright. We do have fun, and at least I'm not always the youngest," said Morgan. "Perhaps your mother might send you as well. My parents think boarding school is just the thing to make good upstanding citizens out of us."

"I go to this fussy little school at Birtle, and none of the girls like ponies or ride. The current craze is for knitting. It's really dull," said Lavender.

"Well, we do a lot of games at our school. Lacrosse is the favourite. There's a lot of running around in freezing cold weather," said Morgan. "They are talking about letting girls bring their ponies and keep them at the riding stables near the school, but that would be the absolute end! I like school because it means I can get away from the total horsiness of home."

They went back to the house, and Morgan led Lavender up a steep staircase to the second storey.

"This place is so enormous. I don't know how you can find your way. I feel like I need a ball of string to unravel as I go, so I can get back to where I started," said Lavender.

Their tea was served in the old nursery with Miss Penwith, the retired nanny. She had brought up all the children and now enjoyed a comfortable retirement in the rooms which had once been the domain of her working life. She was soft and curvy, like a pile of comfortable pillows with a smiling rosy-cheeked face and silver hair pulled back into a bun. Although she had a rather indeterminate and unremarkable face, her eyes were a clear searching blue that seemed to look beyond one's countenance to one's very soul.

"Oh Morgan, dear, who is your little friend?" she asked, her eyes alight like a sparrow seeing a handful of particularly delicious breadcrumbs.

"This is Lavender. She has brought her pony Black Boy who used to be the best friend of Rapide."

"What a wonderful reunion!" cried Miss Penwith. "Come and sit down. Ethel has brought up a sumptuous tea for us, and I've had the fire lit. I can feel a tiny chill in the air. Winter is coming."

They sat down to hot buttered crumpets with honey gathered from beehives on the estate and butter made from the small herd of Jersey cows. Then there were doorsteps of bread with a choice of jams and conserves, and rock cakes, with more raisins than cake.

"This is delicious!" said Lavender, forgetting that she was a picky eater and tucking in with gusto.

"Let's show little Lavender some of your drawings, dear," said Miss Penwith when they had all eaten their fill. "My Morgan is the most wonderful artist. I'm sure she is going to be famous one day."

Lavender wondered what it must be like to have such a benevolent carer who had such absolute faith in one's abilities.

Miss Penwith brought out a pile of drawings that were carefully stored in a set of scratched green-painted drawers behind the rocking horse which was a magnificent dapple grey with a long mane and tail and a real saddle fixed to its back, not just a piece of leather. She laid them out on the table and Lavender was transfixed.

"These are amazing!" she cried. There was a range of birds which had been drawn in exquisite detail, showing every line of feather, beaks and feet so life-like you felt they might just fly off the paper. Then there were squirrels, rabbits, hares and tiny field mice.

"My girl certainly has a gift," said Miss Penwith proudly. "The others might rocket around the country on their horses, but this is something *quite* special."

"Everyone, except Daddy, in this house is horse-blind," said Morgan. "They don't set much store on wildlife unless you can shoot it or chase it. They see no point in putting it down on paper."

"It's like you're one of those naturalists from the time of Queen Victoria," said Lavender, who had just spent a term studying the Victorian era.

They spent an hour looking at the drawings. Miss Penwith produced a book of birds and read out the names of the ones that Morgan had drawn, and Lavender learnt a great deal about the wildlife that lived in Oxfordshire. She began to have a new appreciation of her friend. She even entertained the treasonous thought that perhaps there was more to life than horses. Well, at least for some people.

"What does your mother think of your drawings?" she asked. Aggie seemed like such a kind and understanding person. She couldn't imagine that she didn't rate artistic ability.

"She thinks it's a hobby that I'll grow out of," said Morgan with a tiny grimace. "Mummy is lovely and full of charitable impulse, she does all kinds of good work all over the place, but when it comes to her own children, she is a bit one-eyed."

After they had examined every drawing from the pile, Lavender began to check out the books that lined the shelves on one side of the room. There were some children's classics that didn't feature horses, but most of them were pony books, rows and rows of hardbacks. She opened them and saw that many were first editions, signed by their authors, even dedicated to Aggie and her children.

"This is absolutely extraordinary!" she exclaimed.

"You can borrow anything you want," said Morgan carelessly. Nobody reads them these days.

"That's not entirely true," said Miss Penwith. "Sometimes Royce will come in and look something up. He has got talent too, you know. He writes poetry, and he studied Greats at Lonsdale.

"Does he still live here?" asked Lavender.

"Yes, they all come and go. There's a townhouse in London, in Belgravia and Mercedes goes up there when she's invited to a ball or a party or shopping. Porsche is still at school, but she seems to be scurrying off to

London as much as she can. She's the wild one, you know, only sixteen, but she carries on as if she is twenty-one," said Miss Penwith, a small crease in the centre of her forehead.

"Could we go out to the stables and check on the ponies?" asked Lavender.

"The staff looks after them, but if you like," said Morgan.

Dusk was gathering outside, and a brisk wind blew amongst the trees.

"How many horses have you got here?" asked Lavender.

"I don't know. Mercedes has always got a new one, and then there's the mares and the foals. They'll be bringing them in at night soon, and the foals will be weaned. Porsche is clamouring for some horses of her own, but so far, Mummy says that she must just ride Mercedes' as some of them hardly get worked at all. Austin goes point-to-pointing and he's got this stunning chestnut gelding. Mercedes won't let Austin ride her horses and she's not keen on Porsche, she says that she mucks up their training for cross-country because she's so wild and careless."

"And Royce?" asked Lavender, trying to make sense of this lively and chaotic family.

"He rides, of course. He couldn't get away with not. He's meant to be in training to oversee the estate, so he rides around a lot looking at the fields and the hedges, the herds of cattle and things. He used to be in the pony club like all the others. But now, he gets away with not competing all the time as he's the eldest and a boy. Daddy says he has to learn the ropes on the estate, and Mummy seems to agree."

"Gosh!" said Lavender. Her mind was buzzing.

Porsche was in the stable yard having a heated discussion with an older man, who seemed to be in charge.

"Who is that?" whispered Lavender.

"It's Bert Munro. He's the stable manager. He and Mercedes are the best of friends, but Porsche is always arguing with him," explained Morgan.

"I've got to have Tom drive me down to a show next weekend," Porsche said loudly, in a strident tone.

"No, he's busy with me. We've got to wean the foals and handle them a bit. The mares will have to go up to the far paddock, out of earshot."

"I don't care. He can do all that when we get back," said Porsche petulantly. "It's a big show, and the last of the season, and everyone is going. I have to go, Mummy says."

"Does she indeed," said Bert grimly. He was obviously used to Porsche's demands and wasn't going to cave in just because she used that 'lady of the manor' voice. "I'll talk to your mother and see what she says."

"You do that!" retorted Porsche and strode off, passing the two younger girls without even glancing their way.

Before a kitchen supper, Morgan took Lavender on a whistle-stop tour of the house. There were dozens of rooms, at least six drawing rooms, each with a different colour scheme.

"What is Mercedes like?" Lavender asked curiously as she examined the silver-framed photographs that stood on small tables around the pale-green drawing room with curtains patterned with silver ferns and bamboo.

"She's utterly gorgeous-looking, but it's not just that. She's such a loving person. Just being around her makes you feel good. She has this effect not just on people, but also on horses. It's like she's almost magical."

Lavender thought about this. Although she admired and hugely respected some people, particularly Jill Crewe, she had never met anyone who could be described as magical. Mercedes was royalty, not simply aristocratic as she was an Honourable, but a princess at the top of the equestrian tree. Lavender stared at the black and white image of Mercedes; dark curly hair that framed a softly oval face, with large round eyes that even in a photograph seemed to sparkle with the joy of life. Not only was she featured riding different horses, but also graciously accepting silver cups and other awards. In group photos of smiling, handsome young people, she was easily recognisable. There was indeed something special about her.

During supper in the warm kitchen, Lavender found herself falling asleep over her soup. It had been a huge day, and she could barely stumble down the long labyrinthine corridors back to Morgan's bedroom. Aggie came in to say goodnight, but by then Lavender was sleeping dreamlessly in the spare bed that was placed under the window of the large, lofty bedroom. Silver moonlight shone through the window and illuminated the little sprays of lemon daisies that were dotted over the walls.

"Night-night, Mummy," murmured Morgan.

"Good night, dear," said Aggie, giving her youngest daughter a peck on the cheek, before quietly shutting the door.

Chapter Ten – Trouble in Paradise

The next morning Lavender woke to a diamond-bright dawn. She sat up and yawned and shook herself, thrilled with delight. This was life as it should be. She had imagined they would go for a gorgeous long ride after breakfast but was doomed to be disappointed. Morgan was insisting that they go to her treehouse.

Lavender had to help Morgan pack up a lot of gear, the inevitable morning tea and also a broom, scrubbing brush, rags, a bucket and a container of warm water, which they fetched from the kitchen. Morgan wanted to give it a good clean before she went away to school. Apparently, it was her favourite refuge.

They trundled the wheelbarrow piled high with equipment into the depths of the park to the foot of a large oak tree that must have been at least a hundred years old.

"There's a rope with a bucket tied on it up there. I'll climb up and lower it, and if you can put things in it, I'll hoist them up."

Morgan leapt up through the branches like a goat climbing its favourite tree. Lavender untied the rope that secured the wheelbarrow load, and when the bucket was lowered, she filled it first with cleaning equipment.

After everything had been pulled up, Lavender had to climb. Having had such a sheltered and unexciting childhood, she had never climbed a tree before. It took some time for her to work out the best way up through the sturdy branches. The treehouse was three yards long and two yards wide, with a table and chairs and even a bedframe with the legs cut off short and a mattress that was wrapped in plastic to keep it dry. They brushed away the dirt and wiped the surfaces clean, and by ten o'clock, they were ready to eat their morning tea of rock cakes, homemade caramel fudge, apples and orange cordial.

After such housewifely activity, they were able to enjoy the aesthetic pleasures of their surroundings. The warm breeze was enhanced by the soughing sound of the tree branches and the murmuring song of bees. Through the pattern of leafy branches, the flax-blue sky was a realm of pure bright colour with wisps of cloud-like silvery feathers floating across it.

"Look, there's Porsche and Austin, over there," said Morgan pointing through the trees as the horses and riders hoved into view from the direction of the stables.

"Which horses are they riding?" asked Lavender.

"That's Austin's point-to-point horse," explained Morgan. It was a tall, raking chestnut gelding, at least 17 hh with long legs, a very narrow body, four white socks and a diamond-shaped star on his forehead.

"Has he ridden in many races?" asked Lavender. "I'm not sure what a point-to-point is, like a steeplechase?"

"Yes, that's right. It's for amateur riders, but I think professionals can enter as well, and they just race around, jumping fences and jostling each other in a pack. Sometimes, if someone falls off then the horses behind gallop over them. They have to hunt first and get a certificate from the Master. Austin has won a few races, but he's also had some rather spectacular falls. He's reckless and seems to have no idea of being afraid."

"And that is Porsche, with him. Which horse is she riding?"

"That's a good question," tooted Morgan. "You've hit the nail on the head there. She grew out of Rapide, and now she's entering adult open classes. Mummy has insisted that she ride Mercedes' horses rather than getting her some of her very own. It's just not working out. Mercedes is very possessive and has strong ideas of training, and Porsche's ideas are very different."

"Well, that one is just magnificent," said Lavender, staring in wonder at the dark bay horse. Its coat was gleaming in the morning sunlight, its mane and tail rippling like thin silk ribbons. It was stepping out elegantly, and Porsche was sitting on it as if welded into the saddle.

"That's Banjo. He's Mercedes' pride and joy and her great white hope for Burghley."

"Porsche is certainly a good rider," Lavender said.

"Mercedes is better. She is very technical, and has endless lessons, whereas Porsche thinks she knows it all. She declares that her natural ability will get her to the top," said Morgan.

"Really!" exclaimed Lavender. "For sisters, they are such opposites."

"And I'm different to both of them!" retorted Morgan.

"I have no idea what it would be like to have brothers and sisters," said Lavender.

"You're lucky!" said Morgan feelingly.

They had a grandstand view when Porsche and Austin staged an impromptu steeplechase over the cross-country jumps in the park. They both aimed for the high end of the jumps and took off together, soaring into the air. Austin's horse leapt higher and wider, but the horse Porsche was riding had more speed over the ground.

"It looks dangerous!" exclaimed Lavender, her eyes round in amazement.

"I don't think either of them cares much about safety. They're like the terrible twins. The pair of them have always been getting up to high jinks. Especially compared to Mercedes and Royce, who are both well-behaved and thoughtful people. And I'm the tail end, all on my own," declared Morgan plaintively.

"Oh! Don't say that," said kind-hearted Lavender.

"No, of course not. That's why Mummy wants you staying here. You're the sister of my own age that I never had," replied Morgan.

Lavender looked at her new best friend and realised how wise she was. She seemed to have an in-depth understanding of human beings far beyond her years.

They could hear the approaching thunder of hoofs as the racing horses leapt over each of the post-and-rails, one, two, three; then the hedge, the huge tree trunks and swept around the curve towards the series of water jumps at the stream.

"They can't possibly jump those water jumps side by side," said Lavender feeling as if she were watching a real-life horror movie with disaster approaching. In her mind, she could hear that music that was always played when the exciting climax of the film was about to happen, deungh, deungh, deungh.

"You don't know Porsche and Austin," said Morgan grimly. "You might want to shut your eyes in case there is a terrible scene with mangled bleeding horses in the water."

"They could separate after they jump into the water, and one go over the single fence, and the other swing left over the bounce," suggested Lavender hopefully.

"I think you're rather over-rating the good sense of my siblings," said Morgan in a knowing voice.

She was right. They jumped in tandem over the fence into the water and four strides across the gravelly bottom of the little lake, and then they swung left. Porsche was driving the beautiful bay horse to outrun the big chestnut so that they could jump the narrow bounce fence ahead of them, but Austin wasn't giving her an inch.

They leapt together, but Austin's horse shouldered the bay, so Porsche was forced to jump the upright stake, which was a good eighteen inches higher than the rail. Her horse caught one of his hind legs on the post and tipped over with a crashing fall, throwing her clear across the park.

"Oh no!" bleated Lavender. Morgan was already leaping down through the branches to go and help. Lavender clumsily climbed down behind her, gasping in distress.

They made it to the bay horse as Porsche groggily rose from the ground and began stumbling back. At the same moment, a tall slim woman was flying towards them, covering the ground in long strides.

"It's Mercedes!" said Morgan. "There is going to be hell to pay for this!"

Austin had looked over his shoulder and, seeing the disaster had come cantering back. He leapt off his horse, who stood there blowing, his flanks heaving, watching the group of humans huddled around the still mass of his stablemate.

"I think he's broken his leg," said Morgan in horrified tones. Lavender realised then that although her friend wasn't keen on actually riding, she was full of kindness towards the horses themselves.

The bay horse's near hind leg was twisted at an impossible angle, and his large dark eyes were filled with pain.

"I'll go back to the house and call the vet," said Austin, assessing the situation quickly. He turned and ran back to his horse, vaulted on and was flying across the park before Mercedes got to them. Lavender averted her eyes. She was sickened by the horse's agony. She almost resolved on the spot never to jump a pony again if this might be the outcome.

"You witch! You witch! How could you!" screamed Mercedes as she flung herself upon the bay horse who was twitching in agony on the ground. "Oh, my darling! I know it hurts. You must be brave! Just a little while longer until the vet gets here!"

"It was Austin's fault," said Porsche petulantly, standing several feet away. "He pushed us over to the side of the fence, and the upright caught him."

A row from hell broke out. Mercedes' face was contorted with rage and grief and Porsche looked murderous. She refused to take the blame.

"If Mother had bought me my own horses this would never have happened!" she cried. Her china doll face retained no vestige of prettiness as she was flashing defiance, her mouth set in ugly lines. "Anyway, where did you two spring from?" asked Porsche snakily turning towards Morgan and Lavender, "you're sneaking around like characters in a penny dreadful spying on us."

"We were enjoying a morning in my treehouse and had a splendid bird's eye view of your melodrama!" retorted Morgan haughtily. "Don't think you can pin this on us!"

Lavender wasn't quite sure of the logic of this. Was it that Porsche thought her own horse would have been able to leap the upright post? She couldn't see how Porsche was defending what appeared to be the indefensible.

"You over-train your horses, and they can't get themselves out of trouble!" screamed Porsche.

"How dare you!" screeched Mercedes and leapt to her feet and advanced upon Porsche furiously.

At this point, Porsche turned and flung herself away, running through the trees towards the house. Mercedes turned back to her dying horse and cradled his head in her arms, tears streaming down her face.

Lavender and Morgan watched Mercedes' white face and the dark bulk of the heaving horse in horror. Morgan went over to her elder sister and tentatively patted her shoulder. There seemed no words that would fit the occasion.

Henry Thurston arrived within an hour. His Land Rover was flying across the grass with Ann sitting beside him and Austin in the back, showing him where to go. The vehicle screeched to a halt and Henry leapt out with his leather bag and approached swiftly.

"He's broken his leg," said Mercedes sorrowfully. "I know you're going to have to put him down. Please do it quickly."

Henry examined the horse's leg carefully.

"You're right," he said after several minutes.

"Oh darling, I'm so sorry," said Ann, putting her hand on Mercedes' shoulder. "Do you want to come away while he does it."

"No," said Mercedes firmly. "I'll be with him until the end."

Lavender couldn't bear to watch. She knew that if she were to become the horsewoman that she wanted to be, then she should be standing there stalwart, but she just couldn't. It was too hard.

"Perhaps you two could go back to the house and ask someone to organise to bury the horse," said Henry, finding the young girls an excuse to leave the scene. "I assume you'll bury him out here, where he's fallen, or is there a place for the tractor to drag him."

Mercedes shook her head dumbly. She couldn't think.

"Go back and tell someone that arrangements need to be made," said Ann firmly. "I'll stay here with Mercedes. We need to get his tack off," she said, assuming a practical tone.

They walked back towards the house and saw Bert and Tom approaching in one of the Land Rovers.

"They'll help them to organise it," said Morgan. "There's nothing that we can do."

They walked in silence. A beautiful day dashed into a million broken shards of the worst disaster, thought Lavender. Even in horse paradise there was tragedy.

Chapter Eleven – Death at Pevensy Park

The beautiful bay horse was euthanased by Henry, and his body was dragged onto a farm trailer pulled by the tractor to a quiet patch of land down in the fields towards the river where other beloved Pevensy animals were buried. Mercedes had insisted on being there until the dirt was pushed over Banjo's body. Then Ann brought her back up to the house. She was weeping uncontrollably. Aggie arrived home from one of her committee meetings, and Mercedes poured out the tale of woe.

Porsche stormed into the room mid-way through Mercedes' account of events. The younger sister defended herself stoutly. She refused to take any blame. Austin's horse had shouldered them out of the way. Mercedes' horse was ill-trained and hadn't jumped cleverly. And then she even suggested it was the fault of Morgan and her ghastly little ill-bred guttersnipe friend, who had been slithering around like alley cats spying on them.

Lavender overheard the 'ill-bred guttersnipe' comment, and her face was blazing. She was mortified. She remembered her mother's bizarre fashion choice when they had come to lunch and the way her mother spoke, which was so different to the effortlessly cultured tones of the Pevensys.

Aggie listened to this litany of outlandish excuses from Porsche and then turned on her.

"This has got to stop Porsche! You have to start taking responsibility for your actions! Your school reports have been abysmal. They say that you resist all attempts to be educated and that you're a miscreant of the first order. You have been brought up with every privilege and seem oblivious to your obligation to give back something. You will not talk like that about dear Lavender, who has good manners and a sweet nature. You will not ride Mercedes' horses. From now on, I don't think you should ride at all. You're too irresponsible."

Porsche screamed at the top of her voice. It was an ugly and unsettling howl like a wild animal let loose and about to attack its enemies.

"Let's get out of here," whispered Morgan. She and Lavender were standing in the hallway outside the room. They scurried off to the nursery to be soothed by the gentle Miss Penwith, who seemed fully aware of the situation.

"Porsche has always had a fiery nature. She feels as if she can never compete with dear Mercedes, and there is nothing like rivalry between sisters, sometimes an uncontrollable force," she said knowingly.

"If Porsche can't ride anymore, then I can't see that they can make me," said Morgan smugly.

"But what about Rapide? You can't sell him!" exclaimed Lavender in horrified tones.

"Well, there lies the rub. But I've thought of the most fantastic plan," said Morgan. "Don't worry, Lavender. You're going to love it!"

"What?"

"I'm going to persuade Mummy to let Rapide go and stay with you during term time, and you can ride him for me. Over time he'll become your horse. And your mother might stop chuntering about another pony for you. You just have to jump him enough to win some prizes, and it'll be sweet. We'll all live happily ever after."

Lavender saw the beauty of this plan. It was perfect. If it was a Pevensy horse, then her mother could never say a word against it. Rapide and Black Boy could be together again, and she would have two ponies to ride.

At breakfast the next morning, Mercedes' beautiful face was pale, and her eyes red-rimmed. It looked as if she had wept through the night. She asked Lavender and Morgan if they might help her with one of the young horses that she was training. He had been a racehorse but not a very good one and she was retraining him to event. She had thought she might lunge him with a light rider sitting on top, just as an experiment, and reinforcing the verbal commands.

"Oh, that would be great fun, but are you sure he's not going to buck us off," said Lavender.

Morgan was silent. She was happy to sit and watch Lavender being lunged, but she didn't want to be part of any experiment that might mean landing with a thump on the ground. She had divined her mother's cunning plan that having Lavender around would encourage her to ride more, but she had countered with a much better idea. Lavender could ride, and she would hang around on the edge of the action with her sketchbook. In fact, it was all working out rather well!

They went down to the stables, and Mercedes showed them the gelding on which she wanted to try out this new idea. He had been the most awkward of the batch of young horses and ex-racehorses that had been rejected by racing stables. He was a grey, rangy with a head that looked too large for his body. But this might have been due to his lack of condition, his neck was thin, and his backbone was bumpy.

Lavender thought privately that he was not at all the sort of horse that she had expected Mercedes to own.

"Where did you get him?" she asked.

"He was part of a job lot from the sale yard. Old Ned buys them for the knackers, but I spotted him. I know he's not handsome, rather unprepossessing, but I think there's something about him, some sort of hidden promise," replied Mercedes in her musical voice that tripped up and down the scales with charming intonation.

"Very hidden," muttered Morgan under her breath.

Lavender thought he looked nervous. His eyes rolled and his ears swivelled. He was looking around anxiously. He was not only plain but seemed unhappy and even scared.

"We need to inspire him with more confidence, and I'm sure he'll grow into himself," said Mercedes.

"You're dreaming," muttered Morgan again.

"Morgan, sweetie-pie, I'm the resident horse expert, not you," said Mercedes laughing at her kid sister. "If you had your way, you'd never come near the stables again."

"True," said Morgan. "But somewhere along the way, I've picked up some sense of horses, and what they're about and that one doesn't look at all promising to me."

Lavender looked from Mercedes to Morgan and back again. She didn't know what to think. Of course, Mercedes was the shining star of the equestrian competition world, and Morgan was less than half-hearted when it came to riding, but somehow she thought that Morgan might have got it right in judging this poor wreck of an animal.

Undaunted by Morgan's negativity, Mercedes slipped the lunging head collar over his head. It had a large padded noseband to encourage the horse to lower his head with three metal rings so that the lunging rein could be attached to the top of the nose or one on either side. The side rings could also be used for side reins. Then she carefully fitted a thickly padded saddle blanket over his bony back and put on an old leather saddle with generous knee pads, presumably to help the rider stay in the saddle in case of any wild behaviour.

"I won't put on stirrups if you don't mind," said Mercedes addressing Lavender, and pointedly ignoring Morgan. "That way, if you do come off, and I'm sure you won't, there'll be no chance of you getting your foot stuck in the iron. Also, they won't be flapping around and making him flighty."

"I'm glad you're worried about the wretched horse getting flighty. What about Lavender? None of this is going to inspire her with confidence," said Morgan.

"Oh, Morgan, stop it," said Mercedes, reaching out and ruffling her little sister's hair, "you're just too funny."

"And you're just too patronising," retorted Morgan, but she was grinning.

"The horse is called Mangala, but I call him Manny for short. I thought it rather suited him."

Lavender screwed up her eyes and looked at him. Mangala seemed quite musical and fancy and didn't seem to suit him at all. Manny seemed better. She stepped forward and gently stroked his neck.

"Hello, Manny. You're going to be a good boy, aren't you."

He shivered as she touched him.

"Do you think he's been ill-treated?" she asked. "He doesn't seem to like humans at all."

"Bang on," said Mercedes. "That's exactly what I thought. You've certainly got good instincts."

"Flattery will get you a willing victim every time," said Morgan grimly.

"We're ready now. You've got a hard hat?" said Mercedes. "Let's take him over to the arena."

Manny seemed to suddenly come to life. He danced around, throwing his head in the air.

"I think we'll just attach the side reins, to keep him steady," said Mercedes.

Morgan rolled her eyes.

Then, as they walked across the yard and over to the arena, he began to kick at the girth that was tightened around his middle. He flung himself sideways and tried to rear, but the side reins stopped him throwing his head up into the air.

"I think I'll just lunge him for a while," said Mercedes.

"Have you been on his back yet?" asked Morgan.

"Yes, of course, I have. I wouldn't be putting up Lavender if I hadn't," retorted Mercedes.

"Did he buck?" asked Morgan.

"Well, he did try and get his head down, and twisted around a bit, but I got the better of him. He just needs more work than most young horses at this stage."

"You're such an optimist," said Morgan.

Mercedes lunged him, first at the trot and then as he settled, she flicked the lunge whip and he began to canter. He seemed to have a rudimentary understanding of the voice commands. After about twenty minutes, he was trotting and cantering around without a problem.

"You see, he just needs to settle," said Mercedes in a knowing voice. "You just sit there quietly and draw your pictures, kid. Lavender and I will get on with the serious horsemanship."

Lavender was beginning to wish that she could sit and draw pictures as well, but she didn't want to be shown up in front of Mercedes, whom she admired perhaps more than anyone else she had ever met.

"Will you give Lavender a leg up, Morgan, please," said Mercedes, "so I can hang on to his head."

Lavender was shaking but tried desperately to feign confidence so as not to transmit her nervousness to Manny. She was flung up into the saddle and settled as quietly as she could. The seat of the saddle was rather large for her, but she was thankful that she could clutch the pommel with both hands. At least she didn't have to handle the reins and telegraph her fears through them.

"Walk on," said Mercedes, in her lilting but authoritative voice, and Manny stepped forward. Lavender had never ridden such a tall horse, and he felt so thin beneath her that it was as if she were sitting on a knife edge, not like her beloved solid Black Boy who was so reassuring with his comfortable shoulders and pleasantly arched neck.

"I won't make you rise to the trot without stirrups for too long. So it'll be once round at the trot and then into the canter," said Mercedes.

Lavender's mouth was so dry she couldn't utter a word, but nodded dumbly. She remembered to lift up her head and tried to sink deeper into the saddle. She had done rising to the trot without stirrups and had managed it quite well on Black Boy under the eagle eye of Serena. But, this was quite a different experience.

Manny seemed to rush forward one moment, hop a little, then bounce around. She found it impossible to find a rhythm in his trot. She decided to hang on to the pommel, pulling up as hard as she could and sit there and hope that she managed to stay on until he bounded forward in a canter. He was shaking his head from side to side trying to evade the action of the side reins and then he dropped his inside shoulder and it seemed as if he were going to dissolve into a bucking frenzy.

"Canter on," said Mercedes in a distinctly commanding tone, flicking the lunge whip to reinforce her command. He lurched into a rough canter.

"It's just he's not used to the weight of a rider," said Mercedes, "the jockeys always stand in the stirrups and don't have their weight bearing down on the racehorses' backs." Lavender doubted that it was 'just' that. He seemed to hate having her on his back. He was just beginning to settle a little into a canter stride, and she felt as if she could discern a vague rhythm. Her hands and arms were aching from gripping so tightly, and she consciously relaxed them a little and tried to swing her hips in time to his stride. Then he flung his head up and skittered in a bounding weird step forward.

"Look! It's one of the little sneaks trying to ride a horse!" screeched a very unpleasant, strident voice.

Porsche was standing at the edge of the arena.

Lavender gasped. She knew that this was unjust. There had been nothing sneaky at all about Morgan and herself having a grandstand view of yesterday's unfortunate accident. Nor had they gone running to Aggie and told tales. But Porsche's sharp words seared into her brain. They obviously unsettled Manny as well, and he leapt into the air, fell with tangled legs and went down onto his knees. Having just loosened her grip on the pommel, Lavender tumbled to the ground, which was thankfully soft and giving.

"Are you alright?" shouted Morgan running towards her as she got to her feet.

"I'm fine. I just wasn't ready for him to fall over."

"You're an absolute witch, you!" Morgan shouted at Porsche, leaping to the defence of her friend. "Lavender is a guest in our house, and if Mummy knew what you had just said, you would be in massive trouble."

"Going to run and tell her," sneered Porsche.

Mercedes didn't enter into this sharp exchange of words. She was too busy trying to regain control of Manny who was running backwards on the end of the lunge rein.

"Doesn't look like your training is working very well today," taunted Porsche.

"Porsche! That is enough! Not another word!" said Aggie who suddenly appeared on the scene and had overheard some of this heated exchange.

"No one needs to tell tales when you make such a disgraceful public exhibition of yourself. You will go to your room now! Your father and I will deal with this."

Porsche's face drained white. For all her bravado she was no match for her mother when it came down to it. She slunk away without another word.

Chapter Twelve – Porsche's Punishment

"Mercedes, I know that you meant this for the best, but I don't think Lavender or Morgan should be put up on that horse. He's not quite right as far as I can see," said Aggie.

"I think you might have a point there," Mercedes conceded. "I'll lead him around for a while to settle him. Then I'll get back up on him myself. We need to establish who is boss, but at the same time not frighten him."

"As you like. I'll send Tom over to watch in case you come off," said Aggie. "Now, Morgan and Lavender, perhaps that's enough of training half-broken ex-racehorses for this morning. Royce is driving over to check the mares that have been separated from their foals. Perhaps you could go with him."

"I would love to see the mares!" said Lavender. Morgan shrugged her shoulders slightly but nodded in agreement.

"Go back to the stable yard. He's there now, putting some feed into the Land Rover," said Aggie.

Lavender and Morgan spent the morning with Royce. He was very quietly spoken, civilised to the core. He and Porsche were like oil and water. Lavender wondered how a brother and sister with the same parents and upbringing could be so different. Morgan persuaded him to recite something he had written lately. Finally, he came out with a single line.

My lips burn on the name, like a seraph's kiss.

"What's a seraph?" asked Morgan. "Is it one of those beetles that eat you alive in the Egyptian pyramids?"

"No," he said, smiling at her fondly. "That's a scarab beetle. A seraph is a type of angel, the highest order of angels in a hierarchy of nine. It is a being of light, order and purity. But you were right about the Middle Eastern reference."

"Gosh!" said Lavender. She had never met anyone else who talked like this. She wondered what it might be like living inside Royce's head. It seemed strange that he was going to spend his life as a farmer. Well, sort of a farmer, obviously he would have men to do a lot of the hard work.

The three of them leaned on the wooden fence and gazed at the mares. They were sleek, round and extremely well-bred. They were not settled as they had only just been separated from their foals. They raised their heads and neighed in the direction of the stables where the foals were incarcerated in pairs in the roomiest of loose boxes.

The girls helped Royce carry half buckets of chaff with just a dribble of oats. Putting the buckets at a distance so the mares could eat without too much squabbling. They were not starving, but Lavender found it a little scary, so many big horse bodies and hoofs and the odd bared teeth and waving head at the sight of the food.

"Not too many oats, no protein as we want their milk to dry up," said Royce knowledgeably. "They'll have forgotten all about their progeny by next week. I always find it amazing that the majority of mares don't even recognise their foals in later life."

The three of them got back in time for lunch which was being served in the garden, to make the most of the last of the summer days. The table and chairs were placed next to Aggie's rose garden, which was the best in the district, with blooms of every colour, ranging from cream through to tangerine and lemon to the deepest black crimson.

Porsche had been banished to her room and was sent up a tray. The rest of them settled in their chairs as a very lively exchange of views between Aggie, Louis and Mercedes flashed back and forth across the table. The two young girls took their lead from Royce, who was silently tucking into sliced ham, cheese, salad and doorsteps of home-baked bread.

"Banjo was my favourite horse, and also my best. He was the one that I thought would possibly carry me to victory at Burghley in the near future," said Mercedes, sniffing dolefully. "Do you think Porsche did it deliberately?"

"No, dear. Perhaps she chose to ride him because he was your best horse, but I don't think she deliberately maimed him," said Aggie.

"It's a bad business," said Louis, shaking his head sadly.

"We've got to do something about Porsche. You know the headmistress has told me that she's on her last chance, and if we took her away somewhere else, there would be a sigh of universal relief in the staff room," said Aggie.

"She can't ride any more of my horses. I won't stand for it. Even if I have to sell some of them because there's too many just for me. I can't have her anywhere near them," said Mercedes emphatically.

"I agree you've somehow collected too many," said Aggie. "But it's as much my fault as yours. I've always believed you can't have too many horses, but I think that's not quite true. Do you think there might be one that we could give to Porsche for her own with the stricture that she goes nowhere near any of the others?"

"You could give her Manny. He might teach her a few lessons," suggested Morgan.

Mercedes and Aggie turned to look at her in astonishment.

"You know I think you might be right," said Aggie. He's nothing to look at, totally green and as skittish as Porsche herself. They might just do each other good."

"Poor Manny. I don't think it's fair on him," said Mercedes.

"I think Porsche should be pulled out of boarding school. She gets away with murder there. She can go to the local high school and look after her horse. We've got to do something with her now before she gets any worse," said Louis.

"Louis!" said Aggie in shock. "That's not like you at all!"

"Sometimes, I do have to put my foot down," he said apologetically. "She can have the use of the old stable next to the Primrose rental cottage, we'll supply her with straw and feed, and she can muck out for herself. We'll make sure that the staff don't help her, especially Tom. She's got him wrapped around her little finger."

"You know I think that is a good course of action," said Aggie. "It might just shake her out of her stupid arrogance having grown up with everything on a plate."

"Do you look after your own pony, Lavender?" asked Louis.

"Yes, I do. Sometimes Mummy gets the gardener to help me, but he gets very grumpy. He says it's not his job," said Lavender. "But I love doing it myself. Black Boy is my best friend. I wouldn't mind moving into the stable with him," she added confidingly.

Morgan saw her opening. Now was the moment to suggest her master plan.

"What if you had two ponies?" she asked innocently.

"That might be difficult, with the days being so short and school," replied Lavender carefully. She didn't want to stop Morgan from broaching her idea.

"You could get that girl, Ruby, from the riding school. She could help," replied Morgan innocently.

Aggie shot her youngest daughter a sharp look.

"What are you up to, Morgan?" she asked.

"I was thinking," said Morgan in an innocent dreamy voice. "Now that Black Boy and Rapide have found each other again, perhaps Rapide could stay at Lavender's while I'm away at school. There's that big hunter trials coming up at Blossom Park. Perhaps she could enter him there."

Her suggestion hung in the air. Aggie was astonished. It was usually her that came up with ideas for improving the lives of others. Morgan was more her daughter than she had imagined.

"What would you think of such an idea?" she asked Lavender.

"If you thought it was suitable, then I would love it," said Lavender. "It might stop Mummy's idea of getting me a show pony and selling Black Boy."

"I'll think it over. Of course, your parents would have to agree."

Lavender didn't say out loud the obvious point that her mother would go along with anything the Duchess suggested. Even the idea of Ruby hanging around would be acceptable if Aggie thought it was a good idea.

After lunch, Lavender and Morgan took Black Boy and Rapide for a walk out into the fields. They ambled slowly, letting the ponies graze at particularly juicy clumps of grass. The sky was pearly pale, streaked with low clouds. A cool wind was whispering through the treetops and there was a nostalgic hint of autumn in the air.

"If your mother agrees that you take Rapide then you can ride him at Blossom Park Hunter Trials," said Morgan. "They've been talking about it for weeks now. It's an annual event, arranged by Mrs Whirtley but this year they're rowing the boat out. Goddards Department Store is sponsoring the junior open and the open and the first prize for both classes is a £100 voucher and some very handsome trophies."

"That sounds good," said Lavender, who had no idea what the normal prizes were for such events.

"Porsche has ridden Rapide there in the past. She won the junior open the other year, so there might be some pressure. Or you could ride in the junior novice rider, as you've never competed before," said Morgan. "That might suit you better as it is your first event."

Lavender considered this suggestion. She had enjoyed jumping Black Boy at the shows, and cross-country sounded even more exciting. She watched Rapide and Black Boy now. Their heads were close together, sharing the same clump of particularly delicious grass, their jaws moving in unison.

"There'll be a large contingent from the Birtle Pony Club entered in the pony club teams event at the hunter trials," continued Morgan. "The other big pony club, Ratley River, will be there, and maybe some of the other clubs from further afield."

"How do the teams jump?" asked Lavender.

"They have a special course of very wide jumps, and they jump three in a row. It's quite a spectacle," said Morgan.

"Pony club," said Lavender thoughtfully. "Of course, the Pullein Thompson sisters' books were full of pony club activities. Especially the Noel and Henry series."

"I've only ever read one of those books, *Six Ponies*. It was alright, I suppose, but just too full of technical horsey stuff for me," said Morgan. "Porsche read them all voraciously when she was only nine years old."

The implication was that if Porsche had enjoyed them, then they weren't a good thing. But Lavender had read several of them and adored the detail and had learned a lot.

"Just because Porsche has read them doesn't make them bad," she said defensively.

"I suppose not. There's probably a pile of old Birtle Pony Club uniforms put away. Miss Penwith folds everything up in tissue paper and mothballs. It's one of her things, preserving our old clothes. I think it's having lived through two World Wars has had a big effect on her. She imagines they'll be ready for the next generation," said Morgan. "If you want we could dig you out one that fits you."

"I'm not sure that my mother would like me wearing hand-me-downs," said Lavender uncertainly.

"No, of course not. I didn't mean to imply that you were poor and not able to buy your own clothes," said Morgan apologetically.

"Perhaps there might be something there for Ruby. I'm sure she'd appreciate some proper riding clothes. She's always wearing a dirty pair of plimsolls at the riding school," suggested Lavender. "I hope Mummy agrees to the whole Rapide plan and let's me ask Ruby to help."

"Leave it to my mother. She's a master at persuasion," said Morgan with a sly smile.

"I think I should join the pony club," said Lavender. "Mummy could get to meet some of the other parents. If she can make some friends that way, she can forget about the expensive show pony for me."

"She can go on the committee. That's what my mother does all the time. She has committee meetings coming out of her ears. It means she can rule the roost," said Morgan. "I've vowed never to go near a committee in my whole life."

"You're going to be one of those arty people. You'll have a boyfriend with long hair and playing the guitar," said Lavender smiling at her friend. "World peace and loving everybody."

"And you'll marry a showjumper and spend your life touring the country in a big truck with your little horsey children, collecting scraps of coloured ribbons in the form of rosettes," replied Morgan.

With the future settled so neatly between them, they wandered back to the stables and settled Black Boy and Rapide for the night.

Chapter Thirteen – Rapide and Black Boy Together Again

Porsche didn't appear at breakfast, but when Lavender and Morgan went over to the stables, she was there. She had saddled Manny and was planning to ride him over to the Primrose Cottage stable. Her expression was thunderous, and she flashed a poisonous look at the two younger girls. They stood there silently, watching her mount. Lavender thought that Porsche was very brave, probably to the point of being utterly foolhardy and dangerous for other people and horses around her. Manny looked nervous and was jinking around, his back up, his tail jammed down between his hind legs.

"I hope he bucks her off," muttered Morgan out of the corner of her mouth.

Lavender took several steps backwards. She didn't want to be on the receiving end of flying hoofs.

Porsche vaulted on in one fluid, easy movement.

"How does she do that?" whispered Lavender. "I saw Austin do it yesterday. I'm going to try and teach myself on Black Boy once I get home."

Manny looked surprised to suddenly find himself with a rider onboard. Porsche gathered the reins and closed her legs, and he walked forward obediently.

"Gosh!" muttered Morgan. "Perhaps those two were made for each other."

Aggie appeared through the stable archway.

"Your mother is coming over for tea to pick you up," she said to Lavender. "I'm just going to organise for some things to go over to the stable for Porsche."

She instructed Tom to put some mucking out tools into the back of the Land Rover and a grooming kit.

"I'm glad you trust me to look after Rapide. "

"Of course, dear. I'm sure you're more than capable," said Aggie smoothly.

"What shall we do on our last morning?" asked Lavender, thinking longingly of riding around the park again. She wanted to practise over the cross-country jumps on Rapide now there was the possibility of her jumping at Blossom Park.

"Alright, alright. I know exactly what you're thinking," said Morgan. "We can ride around the park."

They set off together, and Lavender was determined to make the most of this chance to practise over such glorious cross-country jumps. She hoped she would be back here for half-term, but that seemed a long time in the future.

After lunch Morgan suggested they go down to the treehouse, and Lavender agreed. She did like it, the tiny domain that gave them privacy and a sense of being masters of their own fate. Again, they had a bird's eye view of Porsche riding across the jumps. She was up on Manny and cantering around the park, putting him over the more straightforward tree trunks and post-and-rails.

"If he's only just come off the track, you'd think that he wouldn't be ready to jump," said Lavender doubtfully. "Wouldn't he need months of flatwork to get him going properly?"

"I'm not sure that Porsche thinks such rules apply to her," said Morgan grimly.

Manny's head was held down by a very tight running martingale, and he was wearing a pelham bit. Porsche made great use of her whip, and basically, it was her strong riding and utter determination that got Manny around and over the jumps.

"She's probably determined to win the open at Blossom Park in a few weeks," said Morgan disapprovingly. "She'll want to beat Mercedes more than anything."

"I can't imagine being that ambitious," said Lavender. "I mean, I like the idea of competitions and rosettes, but it's hardly the be-all and end-all."

"To Porsche, it is everything. I think she has middle child syndrome," said Morgan knowingly. "Although technically Austin is the middle child of us five, and he couldn't care less what other people think of him."

"I've never heard of 'middle child syndrome'," said Lavender.

"I read it in one of those woman's magazines that Cook reads. I was looking at some of the pictures and came across it," said Morgan.

"Do you think I will end up taking Rapide home with me," said Lavender.

"Leave it to my mother. She is a fixer of gigantic proportions, the mistress of the dance," said Morgan.

Aggie had laid her plans. She had divined upon her first meeting with Evelyn Ellison-Heath that the woman was a crashing bore, without taste or style. It was miraculous that she had produced such an impishly charming child. Perhaps Lavender was adopted? But she wasn't a woman who liked to dwell on the shortcomings of another. Nature and wealth had endowed her with a sumptuous life, and she truly believed that in her turn, she should put her considerable energies into improving the lives of others. She was a keen student of human nature, and it had not been difficult to diagnose Evelyn's unhappiness. She was essentially friendless, which was small wonder, but her desire to be one of the upper classes was probably due to her humble beginnings.

Aggie had decided that they would take tea in a small charming drawing room, that was one of her favourite rooms with an ornate Gothic ceiling, delicate curves in the plasterwork were picked out in gilt that were offset by red silk walls that were shot with gold thread. The room was dominated by paintings of her husband's grandparents wearing their coronation robes. It was an ideal backdrop for this meeting when she was determined to have her own way.

Evelyn arrived punctually. She didn't believe in the notion of being fashionably late. She had dressed more conservatively on this occasion, not clad in the bizarre outfit that she had purchased at Creations. She had gone to Goddards department store and bought a classic cashmere twinset the colour of dusky pink roses matched with a pencil-thin skirt of a subtle tartan of navy-blue, pink and silver.

"Evelyn, my dear, do come in," said Aggie as her guest was ushered into the hall by the butler. "I thought we might have a cosy tea in one of my favourite rooms. Do let me show you. I'm sure you'll love it as much as I do."

The implication was that Evelyn shared Aggie's tastes and viewpoints. Mrs E-H bridled at this suggestion. Her cheeks flushed a rosy pink to match her new knitwear.

They settled down to a choice of teas, Indian or Chinese, and potted meat sandwiches and delicate small shortbreads star-shaped and decorated with crunchy silver balls.

"Dear Morgan has had the most marvellous idea, and I'm sure you'll agree it will suit us all. She thought that now Rapide and Black Boy have found each other again, they might spend some time together."

Mrs E-H nodded in agreement as if the social life of the ponies had always been uppermost in her mind.

"I know that would be a lot of work for Lavender, and I thought perhaps you might employ a young girl called Ruby Swope who has been trained up by Serena at Mrs Darcy's riding school. I've heard that she's come on marvellously and is ready to step into her first job, and you wouldn't need to pay her more than generous pocket money. I do think we need to encourage the young entry, don't you?" said Aggie.

"Yes, of course," said Mrs E-H, who in truth had never given a moment's thought to the 'young entry'. In fact, not having read the Jill books, she had never even heard this expression before.

"I do think it behoves us, as members of our small community to get involved. I find that altruism is my *raison d'être*."

"Oh yes, I quite agree," said Mrs E-H, who had never done one jot of charity work and wasn't quite sure what 'altruism' meant, although it seemed to be doing good. She would have to look it up in the Oxford Dictionary when she got home.

"I was wondering, if you're not too busy, whether you might consider joining the cottage hospital fund-raising committee. I know that they're short-handed and could really do with some new blood, someone full of good ideas and ready to muck in. I know they're thinking of a ball in the spring. A really lavish affair that will raise oodles of lovely cash for the maternity ward."

Put like this, how could Mrs E-H refuse?

"I could certainly be interested," she replied. "I've been looking for something new, just like that," she lied blatantly.

"I'll give your number to dear Mrs Hipkiss, and she can ring you then," said Aggie.

'Mrs Hipkiss, Mrs Hipkiss,' thought Mrs E-H, memorising the name, so she didn't appear clueless when this important personage contacted her.

Aggie twittered on until it was time to go, and Lavender brought down her bag. They all progressed over to the stables to pick up Black Boy and Rapide.

"I told you Mummy would organise it perfectly," whispered Morgan to Lavender, who now found herself with two perfect ponies to ride. She was a little stunned at this turn of events. It seemed that when it came to the Pevensy family, everything was possible, and some of their fairy dust was rubbing off on her.

Rapide and Black Boy rode side by side in the horsebox They were probably wondering if they were going to Pool Cottage. They might also think that Jill would be waiting for them and life would go back to the 'good old days'.

The next step in the master plan was that they should contact Ruby and enlist her to work as their part-time groom and stable hand. Having been effectively primed, Mrs E-H had to think of a suitable wage for the young girl. They went to see Serena and asked if she minded if they poached one of her best helpers. Serena eagerly supported the idea. She was genuinely thrilled that Ruby should have such an opportunity, especially as it would mean exercising the ponies during the week when Lavender had no time as it was dark before she returned home from school.

When they broached the subject to Ruby, she was gobsmacked, and for the first time in her life, momentarily speechless. Her jade-green eyes were shining, and her mouth stretched wide in a monster grin. And wages! She would be able to help her family out, and they could afford some nutritional food that might help build up her mother, who was always poorly with a hacking cough, not helped by countless cigarettes.

"That would be bleedin' fantastic!" she said when she had recovered from her first astonishment. "I would do it for nuffin, but being paid is good, I can 'elp me, Mum, out. She's strugglin' a bit at the moment. But wot about me work 'ere," she asked, turning to Serena.

"I think it is brilliant for you to get a job of work and get paid. I've got a list of girls as long as my arm who want to come and work here in exchange for rides. You deserve it, Ruby, I'm expecting great things of you when you grow up," said Serena reassuringly.

A few days later, Lavender was to have her first Saturday morning lesson on Rapide with Serena. Although Ruby offered to stay behind and give the stables an extra special clean, Lavender insisted that she come too. Ruby rode Black Boy down the road proudly. She enjoyed a view of the world from the back of a pony. It was a completely different perspective. Buoyed up with excitement, she felt like she was looking down at the mere mortals who only had their own two feet to move around. She could see over garden fences, and through the windows of cottages. People stopped and looked and waved. She was like a princess in a parade.

Serena had been apprised of Lavender's planned foray into the world of hunter trials with her first event, the novice rider at Blossom Park. She understood how important it was for her to do well with Rapide and had gone to extra lengths to enter into the spirit of the occasion. She began the lesson with reference to one of Josephine Pullein Thompson's novels.

"I've been reading *One Day Event,* and the first thing they do is adopt what Major Holbrooke calls the Italian canter. They practise going uphill and down at the same pace, first at a trot and then a canter.

"That is such a coincidence," said Lavender laughing in amazement, "I was thinking of trying that out, going uphill and then down at the same steady pace, my stirrups short and leaning forward."

"Oh, well done. Great minds think alike," said Serena.

"I guess the next stage is jumping downhill, but it's a bit scary," said Lavender.

"Well, from what I can gather, Rapide is extremely experienced, so it's just a matter of trying it and seeing how you go," said Serena reassuringly. "Look over there, a gentle slope and that tiny log lying there, right out in the open. He could walk over that log if it came to it. So, try trotting up the hill, along the crest and turn downhill and over the log as if it isn't there."

"Right," said Lavender in a determined voice, but not feeling at all determined inside.

In the book, the riders had to constantly keep their legs on and drive their ponies forward, but Rapide didn't seem to need driving on at all, nor did he rush. He seemed almost perfect, keeping up a balanced pace, his head steady and his movement regular and straight. First, they trotted and then repeated the exercise at the canter.

"Now, let's try a hand gallop," suggested Serena. "You know it's judged on time, so you'd best get used to it, pedal to the metal."

They galloped this time. Lavender felt the wind rushing past her face, and she imagined galloping around a whole course, crowds of people gathered around jumps to watch, cheering and applauding as she and the gallant Rapide leapt effortlessly over each obstacle. They simply flew down the hill and over the log as if it weren't there.

"Now, perhaps a hand gallop and over a couple of proper jumps," suggested Serena. "Try that post-and-rails going up the hill, over the ditch and rail at the top, and down over the narrow gate, that one standing out in the middle of the field all by itself. You must hold him between your hands and legs over the gate as it is narrow, and he's got that naughty glint in his eye. He might just try you out and swerve around it."

Lavender thought about the honour that was to be bestowed upon her, jumping the Pevensys' pony, and she was determined to do it properly. The post-and-rails was only just under three feet but jumping it uphill made it seem at least a foot higher. Then galloping steadily along the top of the hill, she pushed on towards the ditch and rail and successfully negotiated it. Then coming downhill, she was tempted to take a pull and slow down. She resisted this temptation and pressed on. Using both legs strongly and a tighter grip on the reins, she made sure they headed for the middle of the gate, and they were over.

"You're doing tremendously well. He's certainly a good pony, a bit more of a challenge than Bingle, I mean Black Boy," said Serena. "Now, don't forget he needs to be fit, lots of slow work every day and then some long gallops up along the hills beyond the village."

Rapide's training schedule had been worked out by Lavender. Ruby attended the local Chatton school and had time to rush back and ride him before it got dark. On Monday, Wednesday and Friday she would walk and trot him around the lanes, slowly building his fitness. Her favourite afternoons were Tuesday and Thursday when she would ride across Neshbury Common, into the woods and then gallop him to the top of Skerrit Hill. It was pure bliss, galloping like the wind on one of the best ponies ever born. She couldn't quite believe that this had happened to her. She was actually being paid to do what she loved best. With her stirrups short, leaning forward like a jockey, the sound of pounding hoofs on the ground, the wind rushing past her face, she felt as if life could never be more perfect. She always walked him home to cool him down. Bert Munro, the Pevensy stable manager had clipped him with a trace-high clip before he had left, so that he didn't sweat too much. It certainly made grooming him easier.

Morgan had gone back to boarding school but it had been arranged that Mrs E-H take Lavender and Ruby over to Pevensy Park on Sunday afternoon to train over the cross-country jumps. While the Ellison-Heaths were at church Ruby had gone around the field with a wheelbarrow, picking up the ponies' droppings from the week. This was important to keep the grazing clean and sweet-tasting, although in the winter, the grass had very little nutritional value.

After lunch, Black Boy and Rapide were loaded into the horsebox and they all set out. Ruby was quivering with excitement. She had hardly ever jumped, just hopping over the odd low jump at Mrs Darcy's and surreptitiously cantering over a fallen log on Rapide as they had ridden through the woods. Today was going to be the day when she would have a chance to tackle some decent jumps.

It was Ruby's first visit to Pevensy Park and her mouth fell open when they trundled through the gateposts topped by gryphons.

"Coats o' arms!" she exclaimed in amazement, pointing her finger at one of the open wrought iron gates that was pinned back.

"Why yes," replied Lavender, "I didn't notice that before. I guess it's something to do with being a Duke and Duchess."

Ruby gazed in wonder at the splendour of the surroundings. It was so far from her humble abode at Ditching Hollow. The rolling green acres of park, the cross-country jumps as good as anything at Burghley or Badminton, and the stable block that looked like a palace. She had to pinch herself to make sure she wasn't dreaming. It was as if this magical place would vanish in a puff of smoke.

However, Ruby's first impression of magnificence did pale a little when she was introduced to the Duchess, who insisted on being called Aggie. She was certainly not wearing a sparkling crown or ropes of diamonds slung around her neck. In fact, her hair was sticking out of the careless bun that sat askew at the back of her head and her old jodhpurs looked like they should be in the ragbag.

"You two girls must come and stay at half-term," said Aggie. "We'll put one of you up on Troubadour so you've each got a mount, and the three of you can go out for long rides together. But today Mercedes is going to take you round the course. She's riding one of the ex-racehorses that she's been retraining."

"That is very kind of her," said Lavender.

"Not at all, it's good for the horse to go out in company," replied Aggie.

Ruby was still astounded that she had been included in this training session. Life was becoming more magical by the minute.

"Who is Troubadour?" she asked, amazement not quite leaving her speechless. She always wanted to know everything. Curiosity was her middle name.

"He's the horse that my husband rides on the rare occasion that we ride together. He's a grand old chap, a big solid horse but gentle as they come. He used to be quite a jumper in his time, and I'm sure he could keep up with Black Boy and Rapide. Perhaps Morgan should ride him, she has the longest legs of you three."

Mercedes appeared in the stable yard and Tom led out a brown horse that was jittering and jigging around the yard.

"He looks a handful," said Lavender, remembering how she had fallen off Manny during one of Mercedes' training sessions.

"Evelyn do come and have some tea, while the girls go around the course. Mercedes is accompanying them so she'll make sure they come to no harm," said Aggie.

If it were horse heaven for Lavender and Ruby, it was social heaven for Evelyn.

"I must tell you about my phone call with Mrs Hipkiss, the events they're planning to raise money for the hospital sound so exciting," she said to her revered friend as they walked back through the shrubbery tunnel to the house.

The trio set off around the cross-country course. Ruby felt as if she were bubbling inside with all the excitement of her first proper jumping experience. She had read a number of chapters in various books on 'how to jump' and knew that no matter what one should not pull on the reins halfway over the jump. Black Boy sensed his young rider's fizzing excitement but it did not faze him. He was an old hand at this.

Mercedes set the pace and the brown thoroughbred must have thought that he was back on the race track. He galloped off at a tremendous pace and Mercedes had to turn him in tight circles to slow him down. Lavender hung back and waited until Mercedes had persuaded the big horse to jump the lowest end of the first jump. She headed for the middle of the obstacle and looked back over her shoulder to see Ruby and Black Boy smoothly cantering over the small end of the fence.

"Well done! Ruby!" she called. "You're a natural."

Ruby grinned at her and they kept cantering towards the next jump. They got around the course with no misadventures and Ruby's apple-cheeks were shining.

"Tha' woz the best fing I've ever dun in me life," she exclaimed.

Mercedes recognising a fellow horse-mad compatriot, smiled at her approvingly. "Miss Penwith has looked out some clothes for you," she said. "I'll get Tom to rub down the ponies and you run up to the nursery and see what she has found for you."

Lavender led the way, remembering the route through the long corridors that twisted and turned around the huge house. Miss Penwith was expecting them in the nursery and had arranged the most delicious array of riding clothes on the wooden table. There were small pairs of polished brown jodhpur boots, various jodhpurs in shades of green, brown and beige, shirts in an assortment of colours ranging from plain white, beige, pale blue to bright yellow. Each shirt was laid out with a tie of suitable colour. Then there were several v-necked pullovers of good quality wool, barely worn as far as Ruby could see. Then, wonder of all wonders, an array of small tweed jackets, just like what other children wore at shows.

Ruby stood looking at this collection with her small hands clasped together. Her eyes were darting from one item to another, trying to take in such a wealth of gorgeous riding attire.

"Now let me see dear, you're quite small for your age, aren't you," said Miss Penwith. The elderly woman picked out a small pair of boots, beige jodhpurs, a pale blue shirt and a dark blue tie with a navy-blue jumper. Then she added the most darling of little tweed jackets which was a blend of subtle blues and greys, and to complete the outfit a velvet hard hat.

"Do try this one, dear," she said gently awaking Ruby from her daze. Soon Ruby was parading before them transformed into a very smart show rider.

The boots were a little big, but the coat fitted perfectly as if it had been tailored especially for her small frame.

"Yes, I think that will do very well. Now we know what size you are we can add a couple of pairs of jodhpurs. These ones are a little patched but I think they would do very well for ordinary riding and this coat is gorgeous and it is one size bigger than that blue one so you can grow into it."

Ruby was rendered utterly speechless as this bounty was heaped upon her.

"I don't like to presume, but Morgan said that you had some Birtle Pony Club uniforms," said Lavender.

"Of course, of course. They're in that drawer, perhaps you could have a look and see what you think is suitable," said Miss Penwith, who was busy checking the sizes of various other items on the table.

Lavender discovered a whole collection of bottle green pullovers, green shirts and bright yellow ties in the drawer. She noticed that they were arranged in sizes and wondered at Miss Penwith's devotion to order.

It was decided that Ruby should wear one of her new outfits home, and the other clothes were wrapped in several large brown paper bundles.

"Now, I believe it is time for you to go home," said Miss Penwith, checking the time on a very dainty diamond watch on her wrist, which had been her retirement present from the family.

Again, Lavender led the way through the passageways. Down one dark corridor, they were both startled out of their wits when Porcshe leapt from a shadowy corner and snarled at them, like a feral animal.

Instinctively the young girls shrank back. Lavender half-turned to flee for her life but Ruby grabbed her hand and they stood together facing this enemy.

"Can't make a silk purse from a sow's ear," hissed Porsche and walked towards them menacingly.

Lavender took a step back, but Ruby faced up to the older girl and glared at her defiantly. Then Porsche turned on her heel and slunk away down a narrow corridor that plunged into the bowels of the big house.

Morgan and Lavender then took off like little rockets along the main passageway. They didn't stop running until they were outside and making for the stables, where Mrs E-H and Aggie were chatting, waiting for them.

"That was weird," said Lavender breathlessly.

"She doan seem to like us," said Ruby.

"That's an understatement," replied Lavender.

"You girls didn't have to rush. You look like you've been running from the fires of hell," said Aggie laughing.

Neither of them replied to this. According to the code, that one never told on other children, they remained silent.

"Someone called Ann Derry has rung up and invited you to tea this afternoon," said Mrs E-H to Lavender at breakfast a week later. "Now, who is this woman? She sounded like she knew you?"

"Oh, Mummy! You don't listen. Ann is Jill Crewe's best friend, and she is living at Pool Cottage. Her boyfriend is Henry Thurston, the vet, an old school friend of Royce Pevensy," added Lavender slyly, knowing that this would reassure her mother.

"Oh, yes, of course," trilled Mrs E-H. It was astonishing how easily a network of related friends was building up around them since they had met the Pevensys. She resolved to draw herself a little diagram of how they were all connected. She didn't want to be caught out again, not knowing who was who. She believed that dear Aggie had mentioned a Mrs Derry at some point. Now that might be a connection worth making!

"She seemed to be inviting Rapide and Black Boy, with you and Ruby added in as supplementary guests," said Mrs E-H.

"Yes, of course. She and Jill spent their childhood riding together and having adventures, so Black Boy and Rapide are like her oldest friends. Ann has another of Jill's old horses, an ex-steeplechaser called Black Comedy and also Mrs Darcy's retired pony, Totty, in the field at the cottage," explained Lavender patiently. "Do you remember I told you that Ruby and I led Totty over there a while back?"

Lavender rang Ann, and it was arranged that she and Ruby arrive at Pool Cottage after lunch and they should all go out for a ride. Black Comedy was in training for Henry to ride at the Blossom Park event, so a long hack with a training gallop was the order of the day. The weather was with them, although officially it was autumn now, today was bright and sunny, like a last shot of summer before the real winter set in.

Determined to make a good impression, Lavender and Ruby spent at least an hour grooming Rapide and Black Boy before they set out. They knew from reading the Jill books how important being well turned out was, one of the primary virtues of horsemanship.

"Ya know when you be groomin' on the left, that is the near side, you must use yore left 'and to 'old the brush," said Ruby, who occasionally fell into an instructive mode.

"Oh," said Lavender, who had been using her right hand while grooming on the left. "Why is that?" she asked.

"Becos you 'av to put yore weight behind the brush, put yore shoulder init," said Ruby, "Serena tole me."

"That makes sense. I shall remember in the future," said Lavender, who didn't mind at all that her small friend should be telling her how to do things. Besides, she had other things on her mind. "You know I'm worried that when Black Boy and Rapide get back to Pool Cottage, they might think that they're going back there to live," she said anxiously. She always credited the ponies with the most sensitive of feelings.

"I'm sure they're perfickly 'appy 'ere togevver," said Ruby stoutly. "Them get treated like princes in their own palace. They've got nuffin to complain 'bout."

They rode sedately to Pool Cottage, not breaking into a trot in case the ponies sweated a little and ruined the effects of their thorough grooming. They arrived on time to find Ann saddling up Black Comedy. Despite his rather ugly head and thick scarred legs, he looked sleek and fit.

"I've been trying to get some extra weight on him for weeks now, boiling barley and linseed and a special supplement that they're selling at the produce store," said Ann as she tightened the girth. "I thought we might have a good gallop over the downs today. Have you been up there?"

"No," replied Lavender. "It would be good for Rapide as well. We're entered in the novice rider event. I thought about going straight to the open, but it is my first cross-country event ever."

"Jolly good idea! It makes sense to get some experience under your belt. Rapide should breeze around. He loves jumping across cross-country, but you would know that. Regular little grasshopper he is," said Ann.

They set off together. Clattering down the road. Lavender loved the feeling of being in a cavalcade. She felt like the whole world would watch them in wonder, as they flashed by on their shiny, magnificent steeds, hoofs in marching time on the road.

They cantered over Neshbury Common and trotted through the woods. The ground was thick with fallen leaves, and when they got to the top of a hill they drew to a halt for a moment to survey the countryside. It was a magnificent sight and quite took Lavender's breath away. A whole sweep of country, dove-grey and russet, the white ribbon of road, the smoky, purple woods below them and the patchwork green of the pasture and the chocolate brown of the ploughed land.

"It makes you feel so alive, doesn't it?" exclaimed Ann. "Exultant!"

"Yes, that is the very word," replied Lavender, who was glad that the others shared her feelings.

"It makes me wanna gallop and gallop and nev'r stop," said Ruby.

"Well, Rapide might be up for that, but I've got a feeling that Black Boy might get a bit puffed out," said Ann.

Lavender looked at her. It was the first time someone had said out loud her secret fear. Black Boy was getting older. He was becoming something of an old gentleman who might prefer to take life more steadily. It was good that Ruby, who was thin as a stick and light, was riding him. It made it easier for him, but the truth had to be faced. He wasn't going to be up for riding to win in any open hunter trials event. It was alright for him to do showjumping. Such a round only took a minute, but long gallops over thirty jumps were going to be too much for him these days.

"Do you think Black Boy is getting too old?" she asked Ann

"Not exactly. But he is past his prime, isn't he?" replied Ann slowly and carefully.

"Compared to Rapide he is feeling a bit staid," said Lavender. Then, she was appalled by herself. How could she be so disloyal? She couldn't believe that she was such a traitor!

"I guess it is just the nature of life," said Ann philosophically. "Henry is going to the hunter trials with Black Comedy to compete in the open. His own gallant Dauntless has strained a tendon. Black Comedy probably has more of a chance of winning. You know Jill won a point-to-point with him a while ago before she passed him on to me. Susan Pyke came second. It was the event when she announced her engagement to Barty King."

Lavender could tell from Ann's tone that she didn't think much of Barty. He was just a dull solicitor. In comparison, a vet was quite a catch.

"Mummy was saying something about her going to ride that black horse again. He's called Diablo, which means devil in Spanish," said Lavender.

"Oh! Of course, I forgot that she's your mother's god-daughter," said Ann.

"There's Mercedes, an' Austin, an' Porsche in the open," piped up Ruby, determined not to be left out of the conversation.

"Do you know the Miss Farthingtons? Henry took me round there the other day. They're utterly whacky. Two sisters - they never married, and they love animals. Their place is overflowing with all sorts of creatures and the most utterly intriguing thing - they've got a horse living in their old dining room.

He is rather a magnificent horse, and Serena has been riding him for them. They think that he should make a three-day eventer. He's going to be competing as well but in the novice horse class."

"Why 'av they gotta 'orse in their 'ouse?" asked Ruby, as usual, sharp as a tack and curious as a mountain sheep.

"The stables are falling down and full of rubbish. This horse just dropped in their laps, and they're both frightfully excited about it. They dote on him," replied Ann.

They rode on through the quiet country lanes, trotting over hump-backed stone bridges and past white cottages with pretty late summer flowers in the front gardens until they came to the downs, which rolled away in front of them, a glorious endless galloping place.

"It's like the downs which are in the south of England, where Velvet Brown used to train The Pie," said Lavender.

"Oh! You mean the book *National Velvet*, for a moment I thought you meant a real person," said Ann.

"Well, to me, the people in books are more real. I'll lend you the book if you haven't read it, Ruby. It's a fantastic story."

"I've bin readin' bout, Jill," said Ruby. "She's in books an' she's a real person."

"Yes, you're quite right," tooted Ann. "And Lavender, you're in the books as well, and I'm sure you'll feature in the future Ruby!"

"Jus' fink to be in a real book," said Ruby, who had never thought that would happen to her.

They set off at a steady gallop. Ann took the lead on Black Comedy but kept his pace down to a hand gallop, to give the ponies a chance to keep up. Rapide was eager to go. His muscles bunched and gleamed and he snorted. Lavender was becoming more confident with him. Ruby bobbed along behind with Black Boy, nursing him along. She had heard what had been said about him getting older and didn't push him too much. She let him pick his own speed. They pulled up at the peak of the the tallest hill.

"Why don't you stop here and give Black Boy a breather, and Lavender and I can go full speed down that hill, over the broken stone wall, around the far bush and back again," suggested Ann.

"Sure fing," said Ruby, "we'll jus' walk roun' a bit, so he doan get stiff".

Rapide and Black Comedy set out. They were both as fit as fleas and barrelled along without any problems. They flew over the low stone wall side by side and around the bush. Then Ann pushed her gallant mount on, and he flew past Ruby who was acting as the finishing post, several lengths in front of Rapide.

"I have to let him have that feeling of winning," explained Ann. "It's the meaning of his life."

Lavender was puffed out. Her cheeks flushed. They took the homeward journey slowly and arrived back at the cottage in time for tea. Henry had beaten them back, and he had the kettle on and was setting the table with butter, jam and honey. Ann went to the pantry and found a giant coffee and walnut cake that her mother had brought around for them.

"Darling, how was your day?' Ann asked Henry. "Any delicious gossip to entertain us?"

"It's just as well I'm not a doctor and have to keep patient confidentiality," replied Henry tolerantly. "Your thirst for local news is inexhaustible."

"It's part of my charm," replied Ann, grinning at him.

"Serena is riding the Farthingtons' horse in the novice horse, and also Wendy Mead on her bay gelding, Bright Eyes," replied Henry.

"Well, we already knew that," said Ann impatiently. "Come on, spill! You have that look about you!"

"You know me too well," said Henry ruefully. "I was at the Cholly-Sawcutt yard today and that Gary Horton, you know April's fiancé, is entering on a chestnut gelding that they've only just purchased from a dealer up north. He's a wild card. I only got a glimpse of him as I walked past, but Gary wasn't talking about him much. It was all rather Secret Squirrel."

"Gosh!" said Ann. "Gary is the local showjumping star," she explained to the girls. "He got engaged to April to secure himself the position of manager to the Cholly-Sawcutt stable, now that poor old Captain Cholly-Sawcutt has got dementia."

"I think that is a bit judgmental, Ann dear," said Henry, who always liked to think the best of everyone. "I'm sure he is genuinely fond of April. She's certainly the looker of the three girls now that she has lost weight. The other two are still as round and jolly as they've always been, like big bouncing beach balls."

"They've been engaged forever," said Ann. "They haven't set a date yet, have they?"

"Not that I know of," replied Henry.

"When are you two gettin' 'itched?" asked Ruby, the little elephant in the room.

There was silence, and everyone looked at each other.

"Dear old Henry is taking his time proposing," said Ann easily, with no trace of embarrassment. Henry looked abashed.

"Anyway, I've got to get through my vet science course in Bristol, and that will be years away," she went on.

"I didn't know that you were planning on being a vet as well," said Lavender, trying to veer the conversation away from the state of their relationship.

"Yes, thanks to Henry, I got inspired, and I've been back at college getting the qualifications I need to get entry to university at Bristol," replied Ann.

"Does that mean you will be leaving Pool Cottage?" asked Lavender.

"Yes, I'm not sure what Jill will do. At the moment, it's been a pretty neat arrangement where she can come and stay anytime she wants. She might rent the whole property. I'm not sure that she could find someone else for this shared arrangement," said Ann. "Although someone like Jackie Heath would be good. Perhaps Serena at the riding school?"

"I wish me Mum could rent it," said Ruby wistfully. "We live in a caravan thas fallin' down at Ditchin' 'ollow."

"You should talk to Jill about it," replied Ann, "she'll be calling in here on her way back from the horsemasters course at Porlock Vale. She has to go and fetch her mare Copperplate from Essex, and then she'll stop here on her way up to Scotland for Christmas."

They finished their tea and the two girls rode home before dusk fell. The ponies didn't seem to mind leaving Pool Cottage. They were looking forward to their warm stables, cosy rugs and evening feeds.

Chapter Fifteen – All Roads Lead to Blossom Park

The open event at Blossom Park Horse Trials was to be a hotly contested competition. Many of the serious horse riders in Chatton and beyond were training in earnest. Goddards department store's sponsorship with a handsome trophy and a £100 voucher for the open, and also for the junior open, had generated a lot of local publicity. There had even been a small article in *Horse and Hound* that had reached riders from further afield who were thinking that it might be a suitable warm-up before Burghley.

James Bush was riding his tall raking bay thoroughbred, who galloped like the wind and jumped everything set before him. Although James' lack of judgement and technical expertise meant that he relied on luck and careless courage rather than skill. Henry Thurston was a favourite riding Black Comedy, a horse who had an impressive track record and knew his business galloping over fences, and had been trained to the peak of fitness by Ann. Austin Pevensy was riding his chestnut gelding, which was kept fit by Tom, the groom, while Austin was in Oxford at college. Although Austin and his valiant steed had competed in a number of point-to-points in recent years, they rarely won. But they would give the other competitors a good run for their money and added glamour to the proceedings with their combined dashing good looks and air of aristocracy.

Three deadly serious female contenders, who had a lot to prove, were Mercedes Pevensy, Susan King and Porsche Pevensy. Now that Banjo had had to be put down, Mercedes was putting all her efforts into preparing her second and third best horses. The loss of Banjo had been devastating, not just emotionally, but in terms of her competition career. Now she had to work desperately on Sirius and Sassy Swoop. Sirius was a tall brown and rather serious gelding. There were no mischievous twists and turns in his character. He was undoubtedly handsome, but he lacked presence. Reliable and honest, he was never going to be a star. In contrast, Sassy Swoop was all dash and glamour and she sparkled. She was a beautiful dark dapple grey, although she would get whiter as she aged. Her large dark eyes were fringed with thick black lashes and her perfectly shaped small pointed ears were constantly pricked as she looked out on the world that was full of promise.

Although Susan King had thought of giving up riding once she was married, she had changed her mind. She found that hers was not a state of unalloyed conjugal bliss. She seemed to be subjected to a petty social life having tea with her mother's friends where the primary topics of conversation were food, clothes, operations, royalty, dogs and knitting patterns. It was all cosy middle England and she longed for something more.

Barty was not proving to be the man she had imagined, and living in her uninspiring modern house on the outskirts of Rychester, she felt like a fairy trapped inside a glass bubble looking out on a vibrant world from which she had been excluded. Hearing about the Ellison-Heaths' burgeoning friendship with the Pevensy family had made it all worse. She had dropped some outsize hints that her god-mother might introduce her to Aggie but Mrs E-H seemed to be keeping her newfound friends all for herself.

Susan had decided that she would enter Diablo in the open event. He was her father's devilish black gelding that she had ridden in the Ladies Point-to-Point race against Jill on Black Comedy in the previous year. He was a bad-tempered brute, but he had speed and strength and Susan thought that if only she could win the open she would be welcomed into the Pevensy crowd. Of course, Barty didn't approve of her returning to the world of equestrian competition. He had compressed his thin lips and rebuked her, reminding her that she was now a wife and her place was in the home. But she had argued back impatiently.

"It's the sixties, Barty! Things have changed! Women are not content to be chained to the kitchen sink!"

"I thought we wanted a family," said Barty, probably not because he longed for lovable children but as a means of curbing Susan of what he saw as unfortunate tendencies towards unseemly behaviour.

"Of course, we do," said Susan brusquely. "But perhaps we can have a few more years as a couple. I'm still very young, you know."

She had been haunted by dark thoughts in the still watches of the night when she had woken with Barty snoring beside her. Jill Crewe was off, dashing around the world, having adventures and here she was trapped in a house on an estate with a husband who seemed content to go to work every day, his only ambition to become a partner in the firm of solicitors. She feared that she had made a terrible mistake in marrying Barty, but she could see no easy way out of it. She shied away from the thought of divorce. Not only was it still considered socially unacceptable, but it would be a public admission that she had made a terrible mistake. If only she could get in with the Pevensy crowd, then she would feel as if her life were going somewhere.

The most desperate of the contenders was Porsche. She was determined that through dint of sheer determination that Mangala, the unpromising ex-racehorse who had been foisted upon her as a punishment for the accident with Banjo, could achieve the fastest clear round. Although her horse was eligible for the novice class, she was desperate to prove herself and enter him in the open as well. More than anything, she wanted to beat Mercedes and show her family and the world that she was the better rider.

The wild card entry was Gary Horton mounted on his unknown chestnut gelding. The Cholly-Sawcutt stables had made a big show of secrecy about this entry and had aroused local curiosity to the point where people rode past the yard standing in their stirrups peering over the high walls, trying to catch a glimpse of the mysterious and unknown horse. Gary and April were taking the gelding up to the downs in a horse trailer very early in the morning so that they could train without being observed.

The day before the hunter trials many of the competitors descended on Blossom Park to walk the course. There were maps available for each of the classes, and the numbers of the fences were coloured according to whether they were junior or adult, novice or open, and there was a separate course of much wider jumps for the pony club team event.

Ruby went along with Lavender and her mother, who was kitted out in her latest tweedy outfit. They arrived at the same moment as the contingent from Birtle Pony Club, who poured out of a variety of large cars driven by harried mothers and long-suffering fathers.

"They're here for the teams' event and I suppose a lot of them will be riding in the junior novice or the junior open," said Lavender in a stage whisper. "Do you remember Mummy? We were going to join the pony club. Perhaps you could find the secretary and get the forms for our membership?"

"Of course, dear," said her mother eyeing the children critically. "Are the Pevensys members of the pony club?" This was always her yardstick for desirable activities.

"Oh, yes, they were all members when they were children. Morgan still is, but she refuses to go. She says she hates it. Porsche could still go if she wanted as she's only just turned seventeen, but she thinks she is above such childish things. Just think! Rallies, camps, jumping events. Aggie was on the committee and loved it. Ponies up to her eyes!"

"I canna believe that Morgan doan wanna go!" piped up Ruby in her high-pitched voice. "It soun's like died and gone to 'eaven to me!"

"Look at that man. He looks just like Major Holbrooke," Lavender chipped in, surreptitiously gazing over at a man of military bearing with a shooting stick who looked like he had marched straight out of the pages of a Pullein Thompson pony book.

"Does you 'ave to be in the army to be a Chief Instructor?" chipped in Ruby curiously.

"I think it's tradition, but with things changing, perhaps you could be a Chief Instructor one day," said Lavender smiling at Ruby, who was gazing around with wide-open eyes.

"Lavender, Ruby!" shouted a voice. It was Ann, hanging on the arm of the faithful Henry, having just arrived to walk the course.

"Oh, hello!" called Lavender.

"Evelyn Ellison-Heath", announced her mother, thrusting out her arm to shake hands.

"So good to finally meet you," said Ann, rushing on in her merry fashion. "Oh, what a gorgeous outfit! It looks just like something from 'Creations' where Susan used to work. You're Susan's godmother, aren't you?"

"Yes, that is right," agreed Mrs E-H, taking the compliment at face value.

"I hear that she's riding that black Diablo tomorrow," said Ann, with a mischievous glint in her eyes. "They're going to give Henry a run for his money."

"Well Mercedes has two of her horses entered and of course, Austin," said Mrs E-H, thinking that it was rather presumptuous of Ann not to take into account the Pevensy entries.

"Almost everyone will be here," said Ann. "Except, of course, Jill, who is slaving away at Porlock Vale on her horsemasters course."

"Have you heard from Jill?" asked Lavender. "What's her latest news?"

"She's written such an amusing description of her fellow students, and they seem like a jolly lot. Her roomie is from Texas, and her best chum is a boy from Germany, and there is a very weird girl called Willow Veitch. It's quite an international crowd, I believe," replied Ann.

"Gosh!" said Lavender, "that must be fun for her!"

"Did you know Wendy is riding Bright Eyes in the novice horse tomorrow?" asked Ann, rushing on.

"Yes, Serena told me the other day. I go down there for lessons every Saturday morning. And Serena, is riding the Miss Farthingtons' horse that lives in the dining room," said Lavender.

"And you're riding Rapide of course, but not Black Boy?"

"No, I think he's more suited for showjumping these days," said Lavender, "he's not as spritely as he was, galloping around a course like this might be too much for him."

"You know the Pony Club teams event is a shorter course. He could probably still go in something like that. Oh! look! There's James and Diana Bush!" said Ann, flinging her arm around in greeting to the brother and sister. "Yoohoo!"

"Oh, Ann! How lovely to see you. I don't suppose you're riding tomorrow," said Diana.

"No, no. My competition days are over. I just do my bit training Black Comedy for Henry."

"Well, that will be some serious competition for James on Jago," said Diana. "I'm riding one of his other horses in the novice, he's called Lancaster Bomber, and I'm hoping we don't land in a ditch with a crump. James is determined that this is going to be his season. He's been training like mad for weeks now. I can't help wondering whether poor Jago isn't worn to the bone before the season even starts."

"There's some stiff competition in the open this year, as well as Henry and Black Comedy, Mercedes has her two horses and Austin and Gary Horton on his mystery horse," said Ann.

"Thank goodness I'm only in the novice horse. James has entered another of his young horses, Irish Boy, in the novice as well. He's given me strict instructions just to toddle around. He's so competitive he couldn't bear me to beat him even in the novice on one of his own horses."

"Wendy Mead has got her bay, Bright Eyes in that event as well. It will be a jolly jamboree tomorrow," enthused Ann.

"Yes, I'm packing up a huge hamper, and it will be a party out of the back of Henry's Land Rover," said Ann.

"That will be fun," said Diana. "At least we can enjoy ourselves without being squashed down by serious competition nerves."

"I'm sure Aggie will be having refreshments," said Mrs E-H a little haughtily.

"We'll be able to drift from one party to another," said Ann happily, refusing to acknowledge Evelyn's overtones. She was not interested in petty one upmanship.

Ann, Henry, Diana and James set off in a bunch to walk the course and Evelyn herded together Lavender and Ruby and they followed them ten minutes later. As they marched around, Lavender remembered the advice given to her by Serena, carefully envisaging the approach of each jump and then on the landing, she looked for the next jump and assessed the ground to be covered to get there.

The junior jumps followed the same course as the novice horse and the open but with lower jumps. The obstacles included a fallen log, a substantial hedge, a sharp turn and downhill to a gate, into a dark copse and over a wall and out again, downhill again to the tricky water jumps, a very narrow stile, then turning left over straw bales which had a tarpaulin tied over them, a wall with a drop on the landing side, another wall with a ditch in front of it, then a third again with a ditch on the landing side, an imposing post-and-rails and then up a hill to a stone wall and over a series of post-and-rails set against the side of a hill before a steep climb to the finish on the crest of the hill. Many of the spectators would stand at the top of this hill watching the course spread out before them and cheer in the horse and riders as they galloped through the finish.

Lavender was peering into the depths of the ditch on the landing side of a quite sizeable wall. She was wondering how Rapide was going to know there was a ditch on the other side and take this into account when he leapt. It seemed unfair that it should be arranged in such a way. A ditch on the take-off side was fair enough, but this could be a very unpleasant surprise when one was in the air looking down.

"What do you think, Ruby?" she asked. "How is poor Rapide going to know this is on the landing side?"

"I dunno," said Ruby slowly. She sat astride the wall and looked at the take-off, then looked down into the ditch that was not only hidden but full of green and brown dirty water, long strings of green algae. "I wouldna fancy landin' in that," she added.

Mrs E-H was struggling ahead of them up the slope, and they didn't notice Porsche Pevensy striding up towards them. She was standing at the take-off of the wall looking at the place between the white and the red flags where the open competitors had to jump.

"Oh, hello, Porsche," said Lavender, her voice quavering a little. She was scared of this person who had shown such a bitter dislike of herself and Morgan just because they happened to have viewed the ghastly accident with Banjo. Remembering her manners, she went on, "Porsche Pevensy can I introduce you to my friend, Ruby Swope."

"'Ullo," chirped Ruby, darting a keen glance at this young woman who had so startled them when they had been walking through the dark passageways of the big house. Then, just to show that she wasn't that easily frightened, she added, "you be the one who killed the 'orse."

Porsche glared at her with blazing hate.

"You nasty little gypsy," she cried and lunging at her, she gave her an almighty shove. Ruby had nothing to grab hold of and toppled straight off the wall and into the ditch. For a moment, she was totally submerged in the very smelly, dirty water.

"Oh! Oh!" squeaked Lavender in alarm, thinking that she was going to have to dive in to rescue her. Porsche hurried around the side of the jump, and for a moment, Lavender thought that she was going to be shoved into the ditch as well. She had a sudden vision of herself and Ruby drowning in the ditch and there would be two small coffins to be buried in the churchyard.

Porsche glared at her with hatred and spat like a cat. Then she strode on up the hill. Ruby's little face surfaced. Her hair was wreathed in green strands and she was gasping for air.

"It's freezin'" she cried, her teeth chattering like castanets.

"Grab my hand," said Lavender, bending over the edge of the ditch and extending her arm. She managed to pull her friend out without slipping in herself and Ruby lay in a miserable heap on the wet ground. Lavender pulled off her coat and woollen hat and swaddled the wet, bedraggled stick-thin girl.

"That Porsche, she's a witch," said Ruby, her green eyes glittering strangely in a wet, muddy face. "I canna believe she did that!"

"You said she had killed the horse!" said Lavender. "She's dangerous. You should never have said such a thing!"

"Yore not tellin' me it was me fault!" exclaimed Ruby.

"No, no, of course not. What she did was appalling!"

At that moment, Mrs E-H realised that the girls were left behind. She was somewhat out of breath from the steep climb and didn't feel like walking back down to them.

"Yoo-hoo, Lavender and Ruby! What are you doing? Hurry up!"

"Come on," said Lavender, pulling Ruby to her feet. "Don't tell Mummy what happened. It will cause endless trouble."

"Doan worry, I'm no sneak," said Ruby. "But she's gonna pay, that I canna tell you."

"Oh, my goodness," exclaimed Mrs E-H as she saw Ruby struggling up the slope, dripping with muddy water, festooned by green strands of muck. "What on earth!"

"Ruby fell in the ditch," explained Lavender. "I think we should get her back to the car and home into a warm bath before she gets pneumonia."

Mrs E-H looked around, hoping that no one was going to see such a spectacle. Her first thought was that they were making an awful show of themselves. How embarrassing! Porsche had veered around her and was disappearing further up the hill.

They abandoned walking the course and headed straight back to the car. Mrs E-H was not keen on Ruby spoiling the upholstery and found an old picnic rug in the boot and instructed her to wrap it around herself. They drove back to the house, and Lavender ran Ruby a bath, and Mrs E-H instructed the maid to make her a steaming cup of tea.

Ruby wasn't saying much. She certainly wasn't railing against Porsche.

"Are you sure you're alright?" asked Lavender anxiously.

"Doan worry about me," said Ruby. "I gotta plan. She's gonna pay."

"Oh no, Ruby. Don't do anything. You can't act against the Pevensys. They'll have you locked up in a trice. They're important people, you know," said Lavender fearing for her friend.

"There are more ways to kill a cat," said Ruby darkly. "You'll see. That Porsh' she's gonna wish she never cross'd me!"

Ruby was given some of Lavender's old clothes to wear. She was so slight that they hung on her and she looked like a little scarecrow.

"I'll be back tomorrow mornin' early, to 'elp ya get Rapide ready," Ruby assured her and hurried off down the road.

Lavender was worried. She had no idea what Ruby planned to do and she wished with all her heart that the events of the day could be forgotten by everyone. She had no idea how Ruby could go up against the social power of the Pevensys.

Her mother was entirely oblivious of the developing situation and she did her best to act normally.

"Do you think Rapide is going to be fit enough to gallop all that way?" her mother asked when they were eating supper. "I didn't realise quite how challenging was a cross-country course. I somehow thought it wouldn't be much more than a showjumping round."

"Ruby has been riding him up and down the lanes a lot, building up his fitness during the week," said Lavender, always anxious to talk up her faithful helper, conscious that her mother looked down on the young girl who lived in humble circumstances in Ditching Hollow.

"I'm going to ring Aggie tonight and make sure that we can park next to them tomorrow," said Mrs E-H.

Lavender grimaced. The last thing she wanted was to be anywhere near Porsche tomorrow. She was literally scared to death. She just had to hope that whatever Ruby planned to do would not rock the boat anymore.

Chapter Sixteen – Ruby's Revenge

Early the next morning, Land Rovers and horse trailers, and horseboxes, poured in through the gates of Blossom Park. Competitors and their supporters were setting up their camps, unloading horses and equipment and rushing off to walk the course. An air of excitement and purpose swirled across the green sward. There was a rash of competitors arriving from further afield, and the locals were eyeing up the strangers against whom they would be competing.

Mrs E-H had parked the horsebox in the space that Aggie had proposed and was hurrying around with small buckets marking out a reserved space for the Pevensy horsebox when it arrived. They had said they planned to get there by eight o'clock, but at eight-thirty, there was no sign of them.

"I wonder what has happened to the Pevensys," said Mrs E-H, patrolling the parking area she was guarding for them. "I hope that some fresh disaster has not struck."

Lavender was also worried. Ruby was unusually quiet, but there was an intent expression on her little pixie face, which didn't bode well.

"I'm going to quickly walk around the course again," announced Lavender. "Ruby, will you come with me?"

"No, I'll look after Rapide and groom him again," said Ruby, turning away from her.

Lavender set off, course map in hand. After Ruby's fall in the ditch yesterday, she had lost her focus and they hadn't finished walking the course. She was feeling nervous and forced herself to concentrate, suppressing the creeping feeling that something was amiss.

She got back to the horse truck after memorising every fence, every curve of the course and deciding the way in which she planned to approach each obstacle. Still, the Pevensys hadn't arrived. Her heart sank. She was beset with awful foreboding.

"I wonder if I should walk down to the house and ask them if I could use the phone," fretted Mrs E-H.

"Even if something has happened, what can we do about it?" asked Lavender. "I'm going to go and get my number and see if I can find out where I am in the order of going."

She came back with the number 37, which seemed like an omen, but she couldn't quite explain why. Perhaps it was because it was a prime number.

Ruby had groomed Rapide until every hair on his body lay flat and gleaming. His hoofs were freshly oiled and his saddle and plain snaffle bridle were carefully sitting on a clean blanket on the front seat. Everything was ready to go.

"When are you jumping?" asked Ruby.

"It's the first class and I'm eleventh to go. It starts at ten. I want to be mounted and warming up by ten to ten," she replied.

"I am so worried about the Pevensys!" exclaimed Mrs E-H for the millionth time. I've had at least three other horseboxes trying to park in the space there. I've had to be very firm, explaining that it is reserved for the Duchess of Tolkington!"

"Which is their first event?" asked Lavender.

"I think that Porsche is entering her horse in the novice horse, which is the event after yours, so I suppose eleven o'clock. It's nine-thirty now, and she walked it yesterday, didn't she?"

"Yes," said Ruby, her eyes gleaming.

"So, there's still plenty of time," said Lavender soothingly. "Perhaps they've got a flat tyre or something like that. Tom will be able to change it. If the worst happened, they could take the horses out and ride over."

Wendy Mead came over on her bay mare, Bright Eyes.

"Good luck, Lavender. I'm sure Rapide is going to carry you around without a problem," she called.

"How do you think Bright Eyes will go?" asked Lavender politely.

"He's really still a baby. This is his first-ever event, so I'm just going to take him steadily. For the experience, you know."

"'e be lookin' good," piped up Ruby.

"Yes, I'm rather proud of him. You know he's home-bred, he was born on our farm. So, if anything goes wrong, it's down to my training," said Wendy. "Shall we ride over together? You will be warming Rapide up for the first class, won't you."

At that moment, Diana Bush rode up on Lancaster Bomber, one of James' novices.

"I'm in the novice horse as well," she said to Wendy.

"Well, with that horse of the Miss Farthingtons that Serena is riding, that make's three of us. Perhaps first, second and third," replied Wendy.

"More likely last, second last and third last," replied Diana laughing.

"I can see that James has appropriated all the competitive spirit in your family," said Wendy. "I've got to put up a reasonable show just for the reputation of Mrs Darcy's. I forgot to tell you. She's back!"

"Who's back?" asked Diana.

"Mrs Darcy, just dropped in last night, cool as you like. She's here today, but she didn't come with me. She's jump judging."

"Gosh!" said Diana.

At that moment, the Pevensys' splendid horse truck trundled through the gate.

"They're here! They're here!" shrieked Mrs E-H. She sprinted towards the road to direct them into the space she had reserved for them.

"Well, let's be off to warm up, especially you, Lavender," said Wendy.

"Wait a minnit," said Ruby feverishly. "Ya gotta wait until they unload the 'orses,"

"I'm sure they're perfectly capable of unloading without us all gawping at them," said Diana. She wasn't sure that she liked the way everyone treated the Pevensys as if they were royalty.

"Hang on," said Lavender. "I've forgotten to give Rapide his good-luck lump of sugar."

"His what?" questioned Wendy.

"I just like to give him a lump of sugar before we go out. I feel like it's important to him," said Lavender sheepishly.

"He used to jump perfectly well for Jill, with the lump of sugar *after* the event," said Diana, a little sharply.

"No, no. It's superstition. I imagine that the lump of sugar ritual is more for Lavender's peace of mind," said Wendy soothingly. "You go ahead, dear."

Thus, with the small delay as Lavender found the lumps of sugar that she had carefully wrapped in a napkin and placed in the glove box of the cab of the truck, there were four of them and Mrs E-H standing there to witness the unloading of the Pevensy horses.

As Porsche's event was the novice horse, Mangala had been loaded last and was the first to come down the ramp. Porsche was sitting in the front seat of the truck with a face like thunder and left the unloading to her mother, Mercedes and Tom.

"For a child so gifted and blessed, she's certainly not sweet-tempered," muttered Diana, who had heard the rumours of Porsche's unfortunate temperament.

"Yoo-hoo all!" tooted Aggie as she led Mangala down the ramp. "Now, please, I do beg of you not to laugh. I'm afraid that someone has played a rather mischievous trick upon Porsche, and she's in a foul mood."

This caught the attention of the watching group, and they began to smile as if in reaction to the instruction not to.

Tom had brought out the tack for Mangala and stood by while Aggie pulled off his rug.

They all gasped. It was a sight worth waiting for, and they burst into a spontaneous and collective burst of hilarity.

"'e be green," said Ruby, stating the obvious, like the little boy who announced to the crowd that the King was wearing no clothes.

"He is indeed," said Diana.

"Oh, my goodness!" exclaimed Mrs E-H. "What has happened? Has he caught a virus or something?"

There was a fresh wave of hilarity at this ridiculous idea. Mrs E-H looked around puzzled, completely unaware that she had made a joke.

Mangala stood there, apparently unaware of what an extraordinary sight he presented. His grey coat was indeed coloured a vibrant emerald. It wasn't even a good paint job. The colour had been applied in streaks and swirls, and there were patches under his tummy which were still grey.

"He's like one of those modern abstract paintings," said Wendy. "What on earth happened?"

"I'm afraid that someone got into his box last night. You know that he is stabled at the rental cottage, not in the main stable block, and they've dyed him. He's fine. It won't do him any harm. It's just a bit embarrassing."

"Someone must really have it in for Porsche," said Diana.

At these words, it occurred to Lavender that this had the stamp of Ruby all over it. She glanced over at her little friend, whose merry eyes were glinting, the most enormous grin stretched across her face.

Tom put on a rather large white saddle blanket, but nothing was going to cover up the iridescent colour of Mangala, who seemed happily oblivious to his startling appearance. He was rather perked up, probably thinking he was back at the races and due some interesting action.

A small crowd was gathering at a distance and there were squawks of laughter, ripples of tittering mirth and a few shouted comments.

"He be suffering a fit of jealousy!" shouted someone who fancied themselves a wit.

"Green for go," shouted another.

"Wotcha ya bin feedin' him," said one of the grooms who worked for a big stable that had sent a load of horses down from Norfolk. "It's them Oxfordshire 'orses eatin' the green grass down 'ere."

"None of you are at all funny," said Mercedes tartly, as she led Sirius to the side of the truck to tie him up. "Leave us alone. It's not remotely funny."

"That's very noble of you, dear," said Aggie. "Come on, Porsche! Take a deep breath, get out of that cab and warm up your horse!"

Porsche sat there slumped and motionless. Then she catapulted herself out of the cab and stormed around. Everyone instinctively took a pace or two backwards. Such was the strength of fury that was emanating from her.

"I'm not sure that I would have come," said Wendy, "if that had happened to me."

"Winning today is her only mission in life at the moment," said Lavender quietly. "She's determined to beat Mercedes. I think if everything goes well for them in the novice, then she'll enter in the open as well."

"She must be keen!" exclaimed Diana, "to make such an exhibition of herself."

"Come on, let's go over to the warm-up area," said Wendy decisively. "We've seen enough, and I don't fancy being anywhere near that Porsche when she's in this mood." They rode off in a bunch, but the crowd was gathering, and soon it seemed that half the people on the grounds were standing staring as Porsche mounted.

"I'll go and get your number, dear," said Aggie. "Just keep your head up and take no notice of the ribaldry."

Chapter Seventeen – Jumping for Glory

Lavender was quiet on the ride over to the area where the stewards called in the next competitors. Normally she would have been very nervous, perhaps thinking she would forget the course, that she couldn't ride well enough to do Rapide justice, and all the other hundred worrisome thoughts that besieged a competitor on his or her first-ever cross-country course. But her mind was seething with the thought that this was the work of Ruby. She was afraid that somehow she was going to get caught. Porsche disliked them enough before. Now she would probably kill both of them if she got the chance.

Lavender left the others and trotted off towards the trees, and then cantered back. Rapide felt cheerful and eager. She could feel how much he enjoyed being out jumping surrounded by a cheerful crowd. She tried to go over the course in her mind and wished that she had brought the map in her pocket. She got to the fourth jump, and then the rest of the course was a blank. Hopefully, it would all come back as she was riding. As long as she remembered to jump the fences with the blue numbers. They were the lowest of all the jumps. It was just a matter of counting them as she went.

The loudspeakers crackled into life, and competitors for the novice junior rider were called to present themselves to the stewards. Lavender and Rapide trotted several large circles and went on over. Lavender looked around, and there were a couple of riders who she had seen at Chatton and Chesterton Shows. Most of the other riders were in pony club uniform and she watched them curiously. Some of the ponies were unclipped, roughly groomed with worn old saddles and bridles with thick leather straps that looked more suitable for harness than riding tack. Perhaps these were children who lived on farms, who hunted with the local pack and had been riding before they could walk. She didn't automatically assume that she would do better as she was riding a clipped pony with a forward-cut saddle.

There were other pony clubbers whose mounts looked like miniature racehorses, clipped with gleaming tack, flourishing their hunting whips and shouting out comments to each other.

The steward ticked her name off on his list and told her that she would be eighth to jump at this stage, as three competitors had withdrawn. She was not to wander off. She tried cantering some circles and popped Rapide over the small jump that was provided for practice.

Wendy rode over to talk to her.

"Rapide could jump around this course blindfolded," she said encouragingly.

"Which means that if something goes wrong, it will be all my fault," said Lavender.

"Don't be silly. It's your first cross-country. You should just enjoy yourself. By the way, have you any idea who might have done that to Porsche's horse?" asked Wendy.

"How should I know?" snapped Lavender defensively.

"Well, you're tight with Morgan. You've been over there a lot. I thought you might have more of an idea," replied Wendy, scrutinising Lavender's face. She got the feeling that Lavender wasn't telling all that she knew but shrugged her shoulders. It didn't really matter. Undoubtedly when Ann got here, she would be on a mission to discover the truth of the matter. Ann was like that. She had a keen interest in the goings-on in the district and would root out the truth like an investigative reporter.

"Do you think I should ride as fast as we can go? Or just take it steadily?" asked Lavender, keen to change the subject.

"Winning isn't that important, is it?" asked Wendy.

"Not really. I just want to do my best by Rapide."

"I think you should go steadily, and if you feel like it, then step on the pace. That last gallop up the hill is going to sort out the fit and the unfit," said Wendy. "But I gather that Ruby has been riding him a lot, and he certainly looks well. I don't imagine you'll have any problems."

"Thanks for the advice, Wendy," said Lavender. "I think I'll go over that jump a couple of times and canter a few circles."

"Good luck!" called Wendy as Lavender rode off.

She gathered the reins and spoke encouragingly to Rapide who tossed his head confidently. They jumped the practice jump three more times. The steward was counting down the competitors who were going before her. They shot out of the small fenced area that was the starting box.

"Lavender Ellison-Heath on Rapide, number 37!" called the steward, and she rode forward. Her stirrups felt uneven, the saddle seat hard and slippery. Her stomach was flip-flopping, and she had to remind herself to breathe. It felt as if her future was about to be decided.

"Three, two, one. Go!" said the steward.

Rapide jumped forward into a canter as if he knew better than her how to go about this. They rushed towards the first jump, which was a fallen log, merely a branch in the novice class. It was so small one might trip over it. Then on to the second, a hedge, so friendly and normal that Lavender felt her nerves settle. Rapide was the most confidence-inspiring pony when his heart was in it, and she could feel his enjoyment thrumming through him. She remembered the sharp turn, and they cantered steadily down the slope. She wrapped her legs around Rapide's sides, gripping lightly with her calves. They popped over the gate at the bottom into the darkened copse. She steadied him, which gave them a few seconds for their eyesight to adjust. Through the trees and out over a wall back into the sunshine.

Then the course was laid out before them, and they headed down a hill towards the water jumps, perhaps the most difficult part of the competition, certainly the location where a good bunch of spectators gathered hoping for some dramatic splashy falls. She could see a mass of faces as she approached, ghoul-like in their anticipation of thrills and spills. Rapide was determined not to satisfy their desire for disaster and he leapt across a small post-and-rails into the water, across the little lake and out again.

Now, Lavender began to enjoy herself as much as Rapide, she suddenly understood how so many people were fanatical about jumping across country. There was a controlled freedom, the air rushing past you, each jump a different challenge. She gathered Rapide together as they approached a narrow stile. Over they went, a left-handed turn then an easy jump of straw bales with not a breath of wind to stir the tarpaulin which was tied over the top, across the lowest place in a wall, and she remembered to lean back as there was a drop on the far side and she didn't want to land on Rapide's neck.

Then another wall with a ditch in front meaning they needed a bit of speed so they could make the extra width, followed by a drop fence. She had the sinking sensation of a descending lift as they fell through space, and she let the reins slip through her fingers so that Rapide could stretch out his neck and land cleverly. He kept his balance, and she gathered up the reins, and they turned towards the next jump. Every bit of her felt vitally alive, the red flag on the right, the white on the left beckoning them on.

Then, for no apparent reason, Rapide seemed to go back to his old weird style of cat-jumping, which she had read about in Jill's books, and he got right under a substantial wall and catapulted over it like a helicopter. This seemed to put him off his stride, and she felt the ground crumbling beneath his hoofs as he was too close to the lip of the ditch that fronted the substantial post-and-rails.

"Come on, boy, you can do it," she called to him to encourage him along, and she felt him take heart and they were off again swinging over the rest of the jumps with ease. On the last gallop up the hill to the finish, he wasn't tiring at all, and she leaned forward and rode it like a jockey going up to the finish of the Grand National. They flashed across the line, and she heard a spatter of clapping. They had gone clear. She was sure of it unless, by some awful chance, they had missed a jump. It was a clear round.

She felt a little disappointed as they slowed down, and she walked him around to cool down. It was all over. Several minutes of bursting excitement, now nothing but watching the others and waiting for the presentation at the end of the day when they would discover whether or not they were placed. She should have entered the open, but then again who knows, she might have messed up the more challenging course mightily.

Ruby ran up to her, shouting, "Did ya go clear?"

"Yes, I think so," she replied.

"Ya seemed fast!" said Ruby as she gave Rapide's sweating neck a big hug. "Wot a good boy you are!"

Lavender saw Porsche cantering circles in the exercise ring, Mangala's iridescent green colour blending into the grass over which they moved. She decided not to ask Ruby if she had been involved. If she didn't know, she didn't have to make any confessions. Then she saw the group of people they knew, Wendy on Bright Eyes, Diana on Lancaster Bomber, James on Irish Boy and Serena on the Farthingtons' eye-catching skewbald.

"That is the first time I've seen the famous dining room horse. I didn't even realise he was brown and white," she commented to Ruby, glad to be distracted from the sight of Porsche and Mangala.

"How did you go on Rapide?" sang out Wendy as they approached.

"Oh! Rapide was utterly fantastic! He is the best pony! That is after Black Boy," she added, not wanting to be disloyal to her first favourite.

"Wot's the name of tha' skewerbald?" asked Ruby.

"He's called Patchwork," said Wendy. "It's the most tremendous chance for Serena to actually compete. She's so modest, but she's actually a very good rider."

"Oh, hi, "said Serena walking over. "How did Rapide go? He's certainly looking rather splendid."

"We were clear, I think. That horse you're riding, he's got such strange markings," said Lavender. "His face is like equally split in two halves, one brown, one white, and his tail is two colours as well!"

"Wot's he like to ride?" asked Ruby.

"He's got quite a character," said Serena with a smile, "but then what can you expect from a horse that lives in a dining room!"

Everyone laughed at this. Ann rushed up.

"News! News! Mrs Darcy's back from Wales. Oh! Wendy! You probably know already!"

"Yes, she turned up last night. She didn't say how long she was staying for. I didn't want to ask. I think it's decision time about the riding school. I'm on tenterhooks to see what is going to happen."

"She's a jump judge, and she's sitting by that wall with the ditch on the landing side with Colonel Mottley. You know that retired gentleman who organised for Jill to do the dressage exhibition at Chatton. You don't think there might be romance in the air," suggested Ann, as always looking for the thrilling or romantic potentialities of every event.

The loudspeaker was calling for riders in the novice horse, and there were a multitude of entries. Every serious open rider seemed to have one or two novices that they were bringing on, and it looked like it would go on until lunchtime.

"Come on!" said Ruby to Lavender, "let's get your ole pony settled and then we can camp out at the wotter jump. Mebbe that ole Porschey will fall in the cold wotter!"

They took Rapide back and untacked him, settled him with his rug, hay and water.

"You know you could still enter in the open, dear," said Mrs E-H. "Rapide looks like he might enjoy another round. Look at him! It's as if he's smiling at us!"

Lavender looked at her mother open-mouthed. She had never claimed to be in tune with an equine's feelings before.

"No, I don't think so. He did wonderfully today. Let's leave it at that. I'll enter the open next time."

With that, her mother had to be content.

Ruby and Lavender hurried off to get themselves a good vantage point at the water, hoping that Mrs E-H wouldn't want to come with them. The first of the horses that they knew was Bright Eyes ridden by Wendy. The gelding came galloping down the hill most impressively if in fact, a little impetuously and only just under control.

"You never think about it, but Wendy is a good rider," said Lavender admiringly. "Do you think that she'll get to take over the riding school?"

"I 'eard 'er talkin' to Serena in the office one day, and thas wot she wants," said Ruby, who seemed to have no qualms when it came to eavesdropping.

Bright Eyes had seen the water jump and checked his pace. Wendy was using her legs determinedly, talking to him, cheering him on, but he didn't like the idea of jumping into the water at all. He zig-zagged as they approached the fence, but by dint of sheer determination, Wendy pushed him on. He teetered, then jumped at the last minute and landed heavily on the forehand. Wendy tipped forward, and it looked like she was going to land in the drink, but she managed to push herself up off his neck and with a great flourish of her whip and wildly waving her legs, they got through the water, and Bright Eyes gave an enormous jump to get out again and they were off and away.

"Gosh!" said Lavender, "I don't think I could ever manage to stay on like that!"

"But they will be slow now," said Ruby knowingly, with her eye on who might win, "wasted too much time."

There were two rather spectacular falls after that before Diana hoved into view on Lancaster Bomber. She was riding well.

"You don't think of Diana as a great rider either, because it's James who is always in the limelight, showing off and making a big noise," said Lavender.

"It's them quiet ones, ya gotta wotch!" said Ruby.

The big horse gave an enormous jump into the water, landing with a huge splash.

"Thas a wotter bomb!" said Ruby, her green eyes sparkling.

Then with three enormous bounds, they were leaping out over the exit obstacle and off towards the next fence. James on Irish Boy was hard on their heels and both Lavender and Ruby were rather hoping that he might come a cropper. He was such a skite. Be careful what you wish for as it may come true. Sure enough, Irish Boy seemed to crumple at the knees when he landed in the water, and James fell off with an enormous splash and a loud curse. The girls were laughing out loud, and so were a number of the other spectators. James had to retrieve his hat, and he put it on his head and water cascaded down over his shoulders. He bowed to the audience left and right, carrying off the disaster with aplomb. He managed to grab the sodden reins and led Irish Boy out of the water. Using the second jump as a springboard he was back in the saddle and cantered quietly back towards the start, indicating to the jump judges that he was retiring.

"At leas' 'e gotta sense of 'umour," said Ruby.

"I imagine it's the open that he's desperate to win," said Lavender.

The next horse that they recognised was the Miss Farthingtons' Patchwork. Serena was riding very competently, and he was galloping strongly but under control.

"He looks magnificent!" exclaimed Lavender in suprise. "I thought as he belonged to the old ladies and lived in the dining room he would be sort of a joke!"

"'e's got it all goin' on," said Ruby admiringly.

He leapt neatly into the water, three splashy strides and out again.

"Perhaps they'll win," said Lavender.

"Doan ferget the Green Flash," said Ruby grinning.

They had to wait sometime before Porsche came into view. Mangala's colour hadn't faded. He looked iridescent in the sunlight. Porsche's face was set in a savage mask of determination, and she was so strong in the saddle that she looked like she was welded there.

"You woulda spect him to be mor' orkward," said Ruby.

"Remember what he was like when I rode him," said Lavender.

But Porsche seemed to have transformed him from an awkward, bumbling novice to a jumping and galloping machine. He was moving faster than any of the other horses and was into the water and out of it again in less than a minute.

"She really is a gifted rider," said Lavender wonderingly.

"But not bless'd wiv a 'appy character," said Ruby.

"She'll probably win if she's jumped like that all the way around," said Lavender.

"We won' know till end of day," said Ruby. "Les go back, I'm 'ungry. Yore Mum got lots of food, as usual."

"You're right, I'm starving now I come to think of it," said Lavender, "but let's avoid Porsche. I don't think I could face her right now."

They hurried back to the horse trucks and found Mrs E-H's hamper and dug in, munching on ham and egg sandwiches and then eating a whole packet of chocolate biscuits between them. Other people were also enjoying their lunches around them, and a lot of the novice horses were tied to trucks with rugs and hay or being led around to cool down.

"I think I'll lead Rapide out and find him some nice grass," said Lavender. "It's got to be so boring for him to be tied up for the rest of the day."

"I'll come wiv ya," said Ruby.

They walked through the myriad of parked horseboxes and trailers. Snatches of conversation floated around them as competitors and their helpers tended to the horses, tacked and untacked and discussed other people.

"Just brought the old mare up from grass, thought she might fancy a run, what ho!"

"Would have thought that was more your line of country!"

Then there were comments about Porsche and Mangala.

"That Pevensy girl riding that green horse! Utterly extraordinary, like something out of a pantomime!"

"She goes like stink, no matter what colour the horse is."

"Will you kaindlay stup tucking about that poor girl!"

"Poor girl, my foot!"

"Rilly, this must stup immejetely."

Lavender and Ruby walked past the pony club children, who were clustered together in their own area. Mrs Whirtley, the owner of Blossom Park, was rushing around talking to parents and encouraging the children who were preparing for the open junior event that was on after the novice horse. She had a list of children and a rota for them to work as runners to pick up the results sheets from the jump judges so that scores could be calculated continuously throughout the day.

"Ya gotta join," said Ruby.

"I know, I know," replied Lavender, "and you too. Perhaps Rapide and Black Boy can be in a team together."

"Ya think?" questioned Ruby, "never thought I could jump in a competition!"

"Why not? You're just as good a rider as I am," Lavender declared stoutly.

Some of the children were mounted and trotting large circles, warming up for the junior open event, which looked as if it would be as hotly contested as the open for adults. They were kitted out in their pony club uniforms: bottle green jumpers with matching green shirts and gold-yellow ties for Birtle, bright-red jumpers with white shirts and red ties for Ratley River.

"Wonder which club them are from?" asked Ruby pointing at a small group of riders who were very neatly presented with navy-blue jumpers, pale blue shirts and lemon ties.

"Don't know, someone said there was a team come all the way from Norfolk, perhaps it's them," said Lavender.

They walked the ponies over to a corner of the park where they had a view of some of the jumps in the middle of the course. They watched intently.

"How did ya go, jumpin' down that slope with the rail at th'boddom. Looks like ya could trip o'er it," said Ruby.

"To tell the truth, I can't remember," confessed Lavender, "once I got going, it just sort of happened around me."

They watched the junior riders flying by, leaping walls and post-and-rails. Most of them were in pony club uniform, but then they saw Dougie, who had lessons at Mrs Darcy's.

"He is as ugly as his pony is pretty," commented Lavender.

"Wot's the name o' tha' pony?" asked Ruby.

"I don't know. You should know better than me," replied Lavender.

Dougie was flying. His pony's Arab blood showed in its tail which was streaming out behind it like a banner. Down the hill, over the rail at the bottom, but when he went to leap over the wall something went terribly wrong and the pony stumbled on landing and Dougie went over its head.

"Oh! What bad luck!" said Lavender.

When the last of the junior riders had finished, they could hear the loudspeaker calling for riders of the open event.

"This is the big one," said Lavender. "Come on, let's go down to the exercise arena so we can see them getting ready to go."

"Me money's on Mercedes," said Ruby.

"I hope that Henry will do well. He's such a nice person," said Lavender admiringly.

"You gotta pash on 'im!" taunted Ruby.

"Don't be ridiculous," said Lavender loftily. "I just think he and Ann make such a good couple and Black Comedy is such an honest fellow."

Mercedes was riding first on Sirius, cantering circles and popping over the practice jump, which was now set at three feet. She looked very professional, turned out impeccably. Sirius was neatly plaited and gleaming with a perfect trace-high clip. Aggie was standing watching, holding the reins of the gorgeous Sassy Swoop.

"Don't forget to push him on that steep hill with the stone wall. You know he can be a bit slow and stodgy sometimes," she called to her daughter.

"Got it!" called Mercedes.

Lavender and Ruby watched in admiration.

"I'll never be able to ride like that," said Lavender.

James Bush came into the ring and called out to the steward.

"James Bush on Jago!"

"You're number two to go, after Mercedes," shouted the steward.

"Looks like I'll be on your tail, be ready for me to overtake you," said James, brash and boasting, probably thinking he would impress Mercedes with his bravado.

She smiled at him politely.

"Your horse is looking good," said James, but this compliment wasn't going to make up for his boasting.

Henry rode up on Black Comedy, with Ann walking beside him.

"Oh, Lavender and Ruby, where are you going to watch the action? I thought I might sit up on the hill at the finish. You get a good view of a lot of the course up there," she said.

"We were at the water jump before. Perhaps we should try the finishing line," said Lavender.

Henry tipped his hat respectfully to Mercedes but didn't disturb her warm-up.

"Oh ho, Henry!" called James. "You riding that old plug today!"

Ann bristled. She was devoted to Black Comedy and didn't like the implication that he was a has-been or less than handsome.

"You galoot! He's a better horse than yours any day!" she called to James.

"Look!" said Lavender to Ruby, "There's Aunt Susan riding that big black horse!"

"Is tha' the horse she rode when Jill was on Black Comedy?" asked Ruby.

"I think so. His name is Diablo. He belongs to her father," said Lavender.

Diablo was an impressive coal-black beast with evil, dark shining eyes and a thick, bristling mane and tail. Susan held him on a tight rein and he was cantering sideways, throwing his head up, his back hunched as if he wanted to buck. Susan looked strained and preoccupied with trying to control him. The other riders gave her a wide berth, not wanting to get caught up in any fireworks.

"I wouldn't want to ride him," said Lavender. "I hope she doesn't get hurt."

Austin and Porsche cantered up. He was riding his dashing chestnut gelding called Firefly, lounging carelessly in the saddle, laughing at a private joke he had made to his sister. She grimaced at him. Obviously, her bad temper was still simmering as she sat astride Mangala, who looked as emerald green as he had this morning when they had arrived.

"There's Gary Horton!" cried Ann, pointing to April Cholly-Sawcutt's fiancé, who was walking quietly over with April, May and June beside him. "Looks like all three sisters are here to support him. Hey, April! May! June! Come and tell us about this new horse that everyone has been talking about!" she called out to them.

April sauntered over a large diamond ring flashing on her finger. Her two sisters bounced along behind her.

"He's something pretty special," said April. "What do you think?"

"He's certainly tall. He must be over 17 hh," said Ann, "and lean as a greyhound. What's the story?"

"He's quite a successful steeplechaser, and Gary is thinking about entering some National Hunt races. He fancies his chances over the sticks," said April gloating. She was obviously very proud of her dashing young fiancé. "We paid a fortune for him, and this is just a trial before he goes on to bigger and better things."

"I'm sure we're all very grateful that you've chosen to grace our little local event with your august presences," said Ann, hardly bothering to keep the grin off her face.

"You're as sarky as ever," said April flippantly. "You've got Henry on that old black horse of yours," she commented. "But what about Porsche Pevensy? What's the story with the green horse? Is it some sort of joke? A skin conditioning treatment gone wrong?"

"The horse is literally green with envy at your magnificent steeplechaser. No one really knows. It seems someone played a nasty trick on Porsche. Can't imagine why? She's such a sweet person, never had a malicious thought in her life," said Ann.

"I think I might go and ask her," said April, who had no qualms about fronting up to anyone.

"You're a braver woman than me, Gunga Din," said Ann. "Did you see Susan King is riding that black Diablo?"

"My Gary will win, but who do you think will come second?" asked April.

"Pride comes before a fall, dear April. You know that anything can happen with horses. Anyway, Porsche's horse might be an unfortunate colour, but he went like stink around the novice course, and she's the most determined person I've ever seen."

"Look, there's Clarissa Dandleby, or is she married now? That looks like her betrothed with her," said Ann.

"He's an old man!" scoffed April.

"Well, we can't all have our pick of the most elegant and eligible young horsemen in Britain!" said Ann. "If they're happy together, that's what's important. She told us he was a friend of her father's. His name is Charlie, and he's got a jump racing stable. She seemed pretty happy with the arrangement."

"The steward is calling for Mercedes to get ready to go. We're heading up the hill to the finish to watch. Do you want to come with us?" asked Ann.

"Sure, I'll be there for when Gary gallops in on Red Hornet," said April. "Come on, you two!" she called to her sisters.

They hurried in a group across to the hill. They had a view of the beginning of the course, the first jump, the fallen log, the hedge, the gate at the bottom of the slope and into the copse. They could see the horses coming out, but after that they were out of view until the last few jumps, the post-and-rails with a ditch in front of it, and the stone wall up the last steep slope before the gallop to the finish.

"I've got four stopwatches and May is going to write down the times, so we've got some idea of who is the fastest," said April bossily.

"But you won't know who jumps clear or not," said Ann.

"Obviously, but it will give us some idea at least," replied April.

"I'd rather just watch and enjoy the spectacle," said Ann. "It's hardly as if the results will affect the fate of nations."

"You're not living in the same world as Porsche Pevensy," said June. "From what I've heard, she is so determined to win she'd kill the other competitors."

"That's not exactly a sporting attitude!" retorted Ann.

They watched Mercedes gallop through the start. The handsome brown horse was moving well, his pace steady, his long, low stride eating up the ground. Mercedes sat atop in a perfect position, hardly moving in the saddle, guiding him expertly.

"He's a good horse but they say he'll never win Badminton or Burghley," said April knowledgeably.

"I wouldn't mind a horse like that," said Jackie Heath who had come up to join them. He looks so reliable, like a clockwork horse."

James Bush was the next competitor to start and April clicked on her second stopwatch and instructed May to note down the time. Whereas Mercedes jumped in copybook manner, James was all dash and flourish. Jago was a big, brave horse, but like his rider, he was wild and reckless. True to form, he ran out when it came to jumping into the copse. James clung on, but only just. He obviously had anticipated a refusal.

"He doesn't like jumping into the dark," said Lavender.

"'e doan trust 'is rider," said Ruby sagely.

"You're right about that," said Diana, who had just walked up.

"Write down one refusal for James," April instructed May.

A third rider took off, and April used her third stopwatch.

"Here comes Mercedes. She and Sirius look as neat and perfect as when they set off," said Ann admiringly.

April clicked the stopwatch and told May the time. "Not bad, but I don't think she'll be the fastest."

A few yards beyond the finish line, Aggie went up and took the reins of Sirius, threw a light blanket over his saddle and croup and loosened his girth. She gave Mercedes Sassy Swoop's reins and led the big brown gelding away.

"I adore that Sassy Swoop. She's the prettiest mare I think I've ever seen. Wouldn't you love to breed a foal from her," commented Ann.

"Feeling broody Ann," taunted April.

"You're the one engaged. You should be producing babies before me," said Ann loftily. "I've got years of study to become a vet."

"What a slog," said Diana. "Still, I can't talk. I'm off to college next week to study physiotherapy."

"Really!" said Ann.

"It was my original plan, and I've been dithering around, acting as a stable slave to James. Now I've got to do something serious," explained Diana. "But I'm studying at a college in Oxford, so I don't have to leave home."

"Look, there's James!" shouted Jackie.

Jago was labouring up the last hill, only just managing to heave himself over the high post-and-rails.

"He looks done-in," said Ann.

"Yes, sadly, James hasn't quite mastered the art of getting a horse in tip-top condition. He rides him all the time but not systematically. He lacks self-discipline," said Diana.

"He's had at least one refusal anyway," said April, "so he's out of the running."

"Look, my Henry is about to start. Now, I *know* that Black Comedy is fit. I've been the one trotting around the lanes and galloping up and down hills for weeks," said Ann.

Henry and Black Comedy were not the most glamorous of combinations, but the brave old horse looked confident. He had been doing this all his life. To him, it would just be a walk in the park. They galloped over the fallen log and straight onto the hedge, turned left sharply and down the hill.

"He's going well," said Lavender admiringly. Ruby dug her in the ribs with her elbow and grinned at her.

"I'll be interested to see if he's faster than Mercedes. He's certainly going flat chat," said Ann smugly. Then she began to chant. "Come on, Black Comedy! Come on! Come on!" Her fingers were crossed, and she was jumping up and down with excitement. They all waited for him to come back into view.

"Here he comes!" called Lavender.

April clicked the stopwatch as he galloped through the finish, but Ann didn't wait to see his time. She was running towards him, cheering loudly.

"Did you go clear?" she called.

Henry nodded. "I think so. As long as we didn't take the wrong course, I'm sure we were clear. He felt fast."

Ann threw a light rug over Black Comedy. A sharp afternoon breeze had whipped up, and she didn't want him getting a chill.

"How fast was he?" she called out to April.

"He's faster than Mercedes. He's the fastest so far," said April.

"There's those two terrible Pevensy twins to go," said Diana.

"Are they twins?" asked Jackie.

"No, not really, but they hang around together, egging each other on. Austin is full of fun and jokes, and Porsche has got a dark cloud hanging over her head. Besides wanting to be the world champion rider, she's determined to be a wild child."

"Strange, isn't it. That someone who has led such a charmed life is so unhappy with it," said Jackie. "Most people would think they'd died and gone to heaven to live at Pevensy Park, horse paradise, with nothing unaffordable."

Austin was the first to go on Firefly.

"He'll either do a brilliant round, or he'll be an absolute disaster," said April knowingly.

"You've been studying the form, haven't you?" quipped Diana.

"I know what's going on, if that's what you mean. I make it my business to keep an eye on the competition," said April.

Ann wondered when April had got so uppity. She remembered the days when the three Cholly-Sawcutt girls had been a standing joke.

The steward told Austin to go, but his horse baulked and skittered away down the hill. It took him several moments to turn him around and urge him on over the fallen log.

"Well, that's going to cost him dearly," said April with satisfaction.

Susan King on Diablo was the next to go. She had been quietly trotting circles by herself, quite a distance from the other competitors. She didn't look happy. Her father was there, shouting instructions to her, but there was no sign of Barty. The big black horse looked as bad-tempered as ever, and she was clutching the reins as if her life depended on them. The steward called her over, and they charged through the start. He was like a bull at a gate, but as long as she managed to stay on and steer him over the correct course, they might just be in the running for a place. They were close on Austin's heels when they jumped into the copse. Firefly had been weaving around here and there, and he had only just managed to avoid any refusals, but it didn't bode well for the rest of the course.

The minutes ticked by, and then they both came into view. Susan was in front and seemed to be giving Austin a lead. Both horses had settled. Diablo was happy to lead the way and Firefly was following in his wake.

"Susan seems to be giving Austin a lead," said Ann. "Now that's a turnup for the books."

"Diablo is fast, but the chestnut is completely out of it," said April.

When both of them galloped through the finish Ann asked, "so, who is faster, Henry or Susan?"

"Henry by two seconds, according to my reckoning," said April.

"That's good," said Ann. "I'm not sure that I could bear him to be beaten by dear Susan. Look! Porsche's about to go. You've got to time her. She's probably one of the most serious of the contenders, even if that horse is as green as grass!"

"Oh! Ha! Ha!" mocked Diana. "You're a wit today, Ann!"

Porsche was cantering a few circles and forced Mangala over the practice jump.

"That horse looks terrified. It's as if he knows that if he mucks up, he's literally going to be murdered," said Jackie.

"I hope not!" retorted Diana.

"Like what she done to Banjo!" piped up Ruby, who was not afraid to say what everyone was thinking.

Porsche set off, and it was as if the devil were on her tail. From a standstill to flat chat, she drove Mangala to the extent that he ran blindly, leaping whatever was in front of him. In what seemed like seconds, they jumped into the copse and out again, then they were out of sight.

"If she goes clear she'll be hard to beat," said Ann.

"My Gary is more professional than that and Red Hornet is properly conditioned and fit," said April haughtily.

Ann was wishing that anyone, even Porsche, would beat the ghastly Gary. April was insufferable.

Clarissa was soon to go, mounted on a lean and unremarkable-looking brown horse. Her old man husband was checking her girth and muttering away with last-minute instructions. She was called by the steward and set off at a determined pace. The brown gelding jumped cleanly and galloped in straight lines. She was followed by Mercedes on the delectable Sassy Swoop.

"You know Clarissa might be in with a chance," said Diana thoughtfully.

Next, it was Gary's turn to set out. Red Hornet did look impressive, and his rider was lounging in the saddle as if he were supremely confident that they would win.

"Good luck, my darling!" called April as he set off.

"The Horton on the Hornet," said Ann with a grin.

The pair certainly looked professional. The chestnut gelding was all class, and Ann had to wonder just how much they had paid for him. He certainly wasn't from the bargain basement. Gary was fully in control riding with short stirrups like a jockey. She was hoping against hope that Henry's time would be faster. She didn't want to wish disaster on Gary, just a bit of a slow time!

Porsche was galloping up the hill, pushing Mangala to the utmost limits of his endurance. He was blowing hard, his flanks heaving, and he only just managed to clamber over the high post-and-rails. April clicked the stopwatch and frowned as she looked at it.

"Perhaps I've got it wrong, but that looks like a very quick time," she said, sighing.

"Hopefully, the poor horse will still be breathing by this evening," said Diana sardonically.

It seemed to take ages before Mercedes came through the finish on Sassy Swoop, followed by Clarissa.

"Nothing to worry about there, they're both pretty slow," commented April with satisfaction.

Then, Gary and Red Hornet galloped home with ease and polish, but April didn't look pleased when she looked at his time. No one asked her, and she stalked off to help her fiancé dismount.

The open event was over. Horses were being tended to, led back to camp, untacked, walked around until they cooled down, and riders were telling their supporters how their rounds had gone, jump by jump. April was desperately trying to work out which was the fastest, but somewhere along the way, her stopwatches had got mixed up, and she wasn't sure that she had recorded the correct times.

The last event of the day was the Pony Club teams. The jumps were wider than usual, so all three rider and pony combinations could jump abreast, with no fear that one might be staked on the wings, as had happened to Banjo. Points were awarded not only for a successful jump but also for how well they stayed together.

The navy-blue jumpers' team was easily the best. They looked like they'd been trained as a circus act. There were four teams put up by Birtle, and Lavender recognised Angela with frizzy hair, on the pale palomino pony, Christie, that had been in the lesson at Mrs Darcy's. She was in a trio with a black pony and a chestnut.

"Them not 'xactly colour-matched," said Ruby critically.

They didn't jump well either. Christie was at least a stride or two behind the other two and the black pony swished its tail and laid its ears back at the chestnut who swerved to one side, at one point running out at the jump.

"Rapide and Black Boy could do a lot better than that," said Lavender.

"Surely they could," agreed Ruby with a grin. She and Lavender smiled. They knew what each other was thinking. They just had to find a suitable third pony and they were in with a good chance in the future.

Chapter Eighteen – Winners and Losers

"Everyone to assemble up at the hall at six pm," came over the loudspeaker. "The presentation will be unmounted."

"Well, we could hardly take the horses into the drawing room," tooted Ann.

"That skewbald, Patchwork, is used to his luxury inside dining room accommodation," quipped Jackie.

The competitors were fizzing, trying to work out where they might have been placed, if at all. Horses were loaded ready to go, so they were snug in their transport, out of the cold weather.

"D'ya reck'n ya came anywhere?" Ruby asked Lavender.

"I don't know. Probably not," replied Lavender. "I think Mummy will be disappointed if I don't get a ribbon."

"The Pevensys?" asked Ruby.

"I don't think they would care. They just like it that Rapide is not mouldering away in the field doing nothing."

"Lavender, you must brush your hair," said Mrs E-H. "And put on your riding coat that is hanging in the back of the truck. Just in case, of course."

"Yes, Mummy," said Lavender meekly.

Blossom Park was a large house with high ceilings. Everyone was ushered in through the front hall to a large drawing room where there was a wide collection of chairs: ranging from high-backed dining room chairs to numerous soft sofas and armchairs dotted around in disarray.

"Just make yourself comfortable. Perch wherever. Feel free to sit on the arms of the chairs and squash onto the sofa. Budge up so everyone can fit," said Mrs Whirtley.

The gaggle of Birtle pony clubbers were ensconced in a large sofa, tumbling on top of each other, spilling over the arms and lounging on the floor leaning against it. They were squirming and bickering like a bunch of exuberant puppies. The Ratley River members were lying on cushions nearby, and the Norfolk team sitting in high back chairs a distance away.

Lavender and Ruby entered the room with Aggie and the three Pevensy children.

"Come on, Porsche, let's bag a place on that sofa," said Austin, pulling his sister along. She was looking mulish and unhappy, as usual.

Susan was following in the footsteps of her father, who was large and blustery.

"Oh, look! There's that divine girl who was riding the fearsome black steed who helped to settle Firefly from zig-zagging all over the place."

"Austin, you should be able to control your own horse and not need someone to give you a lead like a tot on a leading rein," snapped Porsche.

"Who is she? Does anyone know her name?" asked Austin.

"Mother, who is that woman with that stout country gentleman over there?" asked Austin.

"I'm not sure. Evelyn dear, who is that?" she asked.

"That's Susan King, my god-daughter," replied Evelyn, amazed that for once she knew someone with whom Aggie was not acquainted.

"You keep our places, just a minute," said Austin, sliding across the room. "Susan, I believe, do come and sit with myself and my sister." He bowed in front of her like an old-fashioned cavalier.

If Susan had been less astonished and more socially adroit, she might have quipped something along the lines of, "with pleasure, dear sir." But she looked at him in astonishment, her china-blue eyes goggling. He took her by the hand, and she allowed herself to be towed along.

"Now my two favourite girls," said Austin, seating himself between Susan and Porsche. Three other people sat on the other end of the sofa, and they were bunched together like bugs in a rug.

"Hi!" said Porsche, leaning around Austin to look at Susan.

"How do you do?" asked Susan, remembering her manners.

"I liked that black horse of yours," said Porsche. "Have you done much with him?"

"I rode him last year at the Grassmere Point-to-Point. He came second in the Ladies race," said Susan.

"That's not bad," said Porsche, with a frown. "You know I haven't ever gone in a point-to-point. Austin rides in them."

"Yes, Firefly can't veer around like a crazy thing when he's galloping in the middle of the pack," said Austin.

The room was full now, and Mrs Whirtley made her way to the front. She gave a little speech, introducing Mr Titchley, the manager of Goddards department store who was to do the presentations. Then, she droned on thanking the jump judges and all the people who had helped to organise the event. Her audience grew restive. Everyone was anxious to hear the results. Finally, she stopped babbling and out came the lists of winners and a big box of rosettes to be awarded. An expectant hush fell.

"The junior novice event," announced Mr Titchley, who was the most unhorsey looking individual in a shiny suit and round spectacles that made him look like an owl.

"Fourth is Jimmy Bywater on Custard," he announced. A clumsy boy stumbled out of the heap of Birtle pony clubbers.

"Go, Jimmy!"

"Congrats!"

"Pudding head and custard," joked one of his chums.

He looked embarrassed but awfully pleased, his face flushed.

"Third, Lavender Ellison-Heath on Rapide," continued Mr Titchley.

Lavender had been sitting on the ground at the feet of Aggie and her mother, who were in high-backed chairs. She was thrilled. Third was more than she had ever expected for her first event.

The Pevensy crowd clapped loudly, Ruby was whooping, and Wendy, Serena, Ann, Diana, James and Jackie all cheered.

"I rode that pony last year," said Porsche to Susan.

"He used to belong to Jill Crewe," replied Susan, unable to keep a tinge of spite out of her voice.

"Yes, I met her. She's one of Ann Derry's crew," said Porsche, with her nose in the air.

"Second, Ellie Burton on Tanglewood." She was one of the Ratley River pony clubbers.

"First, Lettie Tregarth on Cornish Boy."

They all lined up and went forward to receive their rosettes. The whole room clapped and cheered. They stumbled back to their seats, receiving individual congratulations and slaps on the back.

"Next, the novice horse competition," said Mr Titchley.

Silence fell in the room. Porsche sat very still, her body tense. She was fairly certain that she had won, but harsh experience had taught her not to assume too much.

"Fourth, Diana Bush on Lancaster Bomber."

"Oh, well done!" chorused the group sitting with Ann and Henry. Diana blushed furiously and made her way up the front.

"Third, Brooklyn Thatcher on Ragamuffin, second, Georgina Tyndall on Fairytown, and first, Porsche Pevensy on Mangala."

There was a stunned silence and then a burst of applause.

For the first time all day, Porsche looked pleased. She stalked up to the front and thanked the Mr Titchley politely when he presented her with a rosette.

"Oh! Jolly well done!" enthused Susan, who had warmed to Porsche, mainly because she was a Pevensy, but also because she was the favourite sister of the gorgeous Austin.

The pony club team event was next and as predicted the Norfolk team, the Sandringham Pony Club (no less!) won.

"They've probably been coached by the Queen," said Ann, as everyone clapped.

Second was a team from Birtle, third a team from Ratley River and fourth another team from Birtle.

By the time all twelve winners had scrambled up to the front, there was a ruckus going on amongst the audience, shouting and pushing and loudly declaiming the victory of their fellow club members. Once that had been sorted out, and they had each received their rosettes, a hush fell over the room.

The junior open with a lovely silver trophy and a voucher for Goddards was announced and it was won by one of the Norfolk pony clubbers, a tall girl with long black plaits, second was another Norfolk pony clubber, a rather determined-looking boy with short brown hair and a chubby farmer's face, third was one of the Birtle contenders and fourth a whispy little girl who looked as if she would be blown away by a summer breeze.

"Now, the long-awaited results of the open event," said Mrs Whirtley, and in honour of the occasion, Mrs Darcy is going to announce the results.

A roar went up from the crowd. She had taught so many of them to ride and been a pillar of the community in Chatton and Rychester for so long. It was great to have her back.

"Hello all you peoples!" said Mrs Darcy, gruff and robust as ever. "It's good to be back on the old home turf and to see so many of you grown-up and competing with the best. Without further ado, it is my pleasure to announce: fourth, Susan King on Diablo, third, Gary Horton on Red Hornet, second, Henry Thurston on Black Comedy and first, Porsche Pevensy on Mangala."

There were several moments of stunned silence. Mrs Darcy's gruff voice had brooked no suspense, and everyone had to digest the results. Porsche had won the novice and the open on the same horse, which was a mighty achievement! Susan leapt to her feet and pulled Porsche up.

"Oh, well done, you two!" boomed Austin and the three of them had a group hug and jumped up and down a bit.

"Henry, you're second! My hero!" trilled Ann.

"It was you who trained the horse!" replied the modest Henry.

"Well, at least you've won a rosette," said April quietly to Gary, who looked rather crestfallen to have only come third.

Porsche received her voucher for Goddards Department store and a magnificent silvery trophy. Her face was crinkled up in an unaccustomed expression of joy and her eyes shining. She had done it! She had proved herself a better rider than Mercedes and on the most untrained and unlikely of horses. There was no way her parents would be able to deny her anything now. *She* was the star rider of the family!

"Oh! Mercedes! You weren't placed," said Aggie in surprise.

"No, Mummy, it's alright. I didn't go all out. I wanted to make sure we went around correctly, polishing up their technique for the future. But we have to give it to Porsche. I never thought that she would pull it off on Mangala, two firsts! You're going to have to let her come back to the stable yard," said Mercedes.

"I know," said Aggie quietly. "If Mangala had been in the stable yard, no one could have got near him to play such a horrid trick. Let's hope that now Porsche will pull her socks up and start behaving more maturely and decently."

Lavender, who overheard this conversation, thought that was unlikely. As far as she could see, this would only make Porsche more insufferable, arrogant and nasty. Ruby whispered in her ear, "I had bin thinking cochineal for the next event!"

"Oh no!" cried Lavender. "I didn't hear that!" and clapped her hands over her ears.

Mrs Darcy walked back into the crowd and found herself surrounded by Ann, Diana, Jackie, James and Wendy, all throwing questions at her.

"Alright, alright, people. Yes, I'm home for good and I won't be going back to Wales. My sister is now fixed up with a nurse living in and we've made all the arrangements for her. I'm back to my riding school, and it's going to be business as usual."

Wendy's face fell at this announcement.

"But I'm hoping that Wendy is going to become my partner, equal shares, and we'll run it together, and when I'm ready to retire properly, it will be all hers," said Mrs Darcy. A huge cheer went up!

"For she's a jolly good fellow ..." They all sang.

"I had no idea that Mrs Darcy was such a local hero," said Mrs E-H. "Of course, Lavender will probably be getting her lessons from her now that she's back."

"But I want to stick to Serena," said Lavender. "She's a brilliant teacher and she knows me and Black Boy and Rapide."

"We'll see," said her mother, who always felt that they should be getting the best.

There were cups of tea and cakes and sandwiches and everyone crowded around the tables, talking at the top of their voices. Then, suddenly the room emptied. The horses and ponies were standing in the trucks and trailers and longing to be home in their cosy stables. As the vehicles pulled out there were shouted good-byes and 'see you soons' to each other and Blossom Park was quiet. It had been quite a day!

Chapter Nineteen – The Aftermath

Blossom Park Hunter Trials was a turning point in the lives of many of the people and horses. April was determined that Gary was going to make his mark and was looking at a schedule of point-to-points, intending to travel as far as was needed to enter the best events. She was rather hoping that they might get to the Grand National.

Ann and Henry discussed Black Comedy's success on the drive home. They decided that he should be retired from all future competitions. Henry's own horse, Dauntless, had finally recovered from his leg injury, and Ann had volunteered to start getting him fit. Secretly, Ann was wondering if she could bear to move to Bristol to study and spend so many years away from her Chatton friends. They had such a lovely friendship group. If only Jill could come back to live here, then everything would be perfect. She could marry Henry next summer and could always assist him with operations and make his appointments.

Speaking some of her thoughts aloud, Ann said, "Henry, I've just had the most amazing thought. What if Jill could marry Austin Pevensy, then she would be living on our doorstep, and we could live in Pool Cottage."

"Austin Pevensy!" exclaimed Henry in astonishment. "I don't think so!"

"Why not? He's rather dishy-looking and very genial," said Ann.

"Because he's just flash and dance. There's no substance to him. Now Royce, perhaps. But I don't think Jill craves the life of a Duchess."

"But she's got used to living in a castle, with servants. That's a good introduction to a more aristocratic life," argued Ann.

"I think you're underestimating your friend. Jill is one of the most unpretentious women that I've met. Yes, she's taken castle life in her stride, but she seems to enjoy coming back here to the cottage."

"Well, she's going to have to get married eventually, and I do want her settled close to us," said Ann. Henry smiled at her tolerantly. For all Ann's interest in people and supposition about their lives, she did have her blind spots. He had no intention of telling her who he thought Jill would marry. Sometimes chaps had to keep things to themselves.

Diana Bush was to set off to Oxford on the following Monday to study physiotherapy. She was looking forward to doing something for herself. Riding as James' unpaid junior assistant was getting a little tiresome. He was so bossy and annoying. He never praised her, and she knew that she was at least as good as rider as him. Just not ambitious.

At the riding school, there was an air of bustle and excitement. The ponies sensed something in the air, and their eyes were bright, their ears pricked, and they looked around with an air of expectation. Finally, Mrs Darcy had returned. There was what might have been called a staff meeting on Monday morning. Really, it was just a jolly morning tea with a cake and a big discussion of the future. Mrs Darcy and Wendy began writing down the conditions of their partnership so that it was all clear and there would be no misunderstandings or disputes in the future. They assured Serena that her job was safe and gave her a pay rise.

After the meeting, Serena rang the Miss Farthingtons. They were thrilled with Patchwork's debut performance and happily agreed to Serena's idea that he should begin some intensive dressage training as a foundation for his future eventing career.

At Pevensy Park, Mercedes was thinking that neither Sirius nor Sassy Swoop was ever going to become champions, and she needed to find herself another Banjo. Mangala had been reinstated in his former loose box in the main stable complex when they had returned from Blossom Park. Aggie and Louis had told Porsche that she was to be given another mount as her exclusive ride, and they would do everything they could to support her future riding career if she did her bit and got at least reasonable results at school and no more phone calls from the headmistress.

The most fascinating turn of events that occurred because of the hunter trials was that Susan King fell in love. For the first time in her life, she experienced a cataclysmic and soul-shattering state of infatuation. It was nothing like the tepid affection that she had felt upon her first meeting with Barty. When she had sat next to Austin on the sofa at the presentation, her body had awoken, and she felt an electric charge surge through her.

She was entranced by the mere sight of his profile. His nose was noble, almost patrician, straight with small, neat nostrils carved at the correct angle, his mouth, wide and sensuous. She sighed at the thought of how he would kiss. His merry eyes had lines crinkling at the corners, which was utterly charming. His skin was flawless, a golden light tan and his hair a mass of shiny brown curls, longish with perhaps the hint of a bohemian who scorned the middle-class idea of regular haircuts that were acceptable in the office. His beautiful soul shone through his good looks. He found life endlessly amusing and laughed with an open mouth, flashing his gnashers which were aligned in perfect white rows. He had an unapologetic rumbling chuckle. He never seemed to have entertained a negative feeling. He was vibrant with the possibilities of life, and his tall, athletic body felt hard and warm next to her on the sofa.

She had originally thought that a social connection with the Pevensys would lift her life out of stolid respectability that had somehow turned into an existence so crushingly boring that she felt she couldn't breathe. She had had no idea that she would tumble into the abyss of deep emotional quintessential romance that coursed through her mind, soul and body, causing her to thrum with excitement in every way.

She had had a recurring dream since her wedding that she was a radiant unclad spirit tripping down a corridor of trees that shone gold and amber and copper. But now this unlikely vision was replaced by the thought of her creamy peachy skin lying next to the bronzed god-like body of Austin in such a tender, but sensuous embrace that it took away her breath.

After the presentation at Blossom Park, her father had dropped her off at the house on the outskirts of Rychester, and she had floated indoors on a glorious bubble of triumph to be met with the cold, merciless disapprobation of Barty, who had not wanted her to compete. He didn't ask how she had gone, so there wasn't even an attempt at conventional discourse when she would tell him that she had come fourth, which was something of a triumph when you looked at the calibre of riders and horses that had been competing.

She had prepared some cold cuts, salad and bread and butter and left it in the larder. She went in and fetched it out and laid the table for two. Barty at one end and herself at the other, separated not only by the length of the table but by a huge aching and uncomfortable silence. He was at pains to communicate his disapproval. She could see this, his thin lips, his mean little eyes, the sniffy toss of his head, but it was like a distant observation. Her mind was billowing with clouds of love for Austin. She imagined him back at Pevensy Park regaling his family with his own version of Firefly's wayward behaviour and talking up Porsche's triumph. How she wished she could be there with them and not in this cold little house with a mean, thin and unathletic husband who held absolutely no charm for her.

She lay in bed that night, as far away from Barty's rejecting back as possible. She had to see Austin again, as soon as possible, but he would be back at Oxford on Monday. She would pursue a friendship with Porsche that would be the way to go. She liked her. She admired her haughty arrogance and strong spirit, and she was undoubtedly the best rider in the district. Better than Mercedes for all her goody-two-shoes posturing and certainly better than Jill Crewe and any of her gang.

She would have to think of a pretext to visit Porsche and to get in with the family. She hoped no one would think it strange that she should be friends with a seventeen-year-old schoolgirl. Porsche seemed more grown-up than any other schoolgirl she had ever known.

Lavender and Ruby were to join Birtle Pony Club and would attend their first rally at half-term. There had been no discussion about Rapide's future. Secretly, Lavender was hoping that if Aggie ever accepted the fact that Morgan really didn't want a pony, then they might sell him to them. That would settle the second pony question once and for all, and she wouldn't continue to worry about her mother selling Black Boy.

Black Boy and Rapide were whiffling to each other in their adjacent loose boxes. Rapide was telling him all about the hunter trials and the way in which Lavender had ridden. They were content and happy, to be together again was pony bliss.

THE END

www.ingramcontent.com/pod-product-compliance
Lightning Source LLC
Chambersburg PA
CBHW070938250626
47159CB00009B/3302